# Heartland ™

## Sooner or Later

itaire!" Amy exclaimed, pulling the foal up sharply.
it!" Solitaire half-reared. As he came down, one of his
hooves landed squarely on Amy's foot.

w!" Amy cried. Pain and anger blinded her and her
flew up. "You stupid…"

e stopped on the very point of smacking Solitaire's
. The world seemed to stand very still for a moment and
slowly she lowered her arm. She breathed out shakily.
was she thinking of? She'd almost hit a horse!

ny?" She swung round. Grandpa had dropped his fence
s and was hurrying across the field towards her, a look of
ern on his face. "What's going on?"

Read all the books about Heartland:

*Coming Home*
*After the Storm*
*Breaking Free*
*Taking Chances*
*Come What May*
*One Day You'll Know*
*Out of the Darkness*
*Thicker Than Water*
*Every New Day*
*Tomorrow's Promise*
*True Enough*

And look out for...
*Darkest Hour*

# Heartland ™

## Sooner or Later

### Lauren Brooke

SCHOLASTIC

Scholastic Children's Books,
Commonwealth House, 1-19 New Oxford Street,
London WC1A 1NU, UK
a division of Scholastic Ltd
London ~ New York ~ Toronto ~ Sydney ~ Auckland
Mexico City ~ New Delhi ~ Hong Kong

First published in the UK by Scholastic Ltd, 2003
Series created by Working Partners Ltd

ISBN 0 439 98195 6

Typeset by TW Typesetting, Midsomer Norton, Somerset
Printed and bound by Nørhaven Paperback, Viborg, Denmark

6 8 10 9 7 5

To Tan and Bramble, my two special boys. I couldn't have written this book if I hadn't had to say goodbye to you, but if I'd had the choice...

This book is also dedicated to Mark Rashid for his amazing books on working with horses and to Nick, Brian and everyone else at Meadow Lane Veterinary Centre for answering my questions so patiently. Any mistakes are mine but there are many scenes in Heartland that could not have been written without their help. Thank you.

# Chapter One

At five o'clock Amy's alarm clock rang out. Surfacing from a dream, she groped for the "off" button. It couldn't be time to get up yet, could it? She flopped back against her pillows and shut her eyes. *Just a few more minutes*, she thought.

She woke up with a start some time later. What time was it? She looked at her clock. Quarter to six! She was never going to be ready to leave by eight!

Quickly she jumped out of bed and grabbed her jeans from the floor. She pulled on her clothes and, tying her long light-brown hair back in a pony-tail, she ran down the stairs and outside.

*Brush Storm. Braid him. Put his show kit in Ben's trailer. Muck out six stalls.* The list of things to do ran through her mind. As she looked over her horse's door, her heart sank. In the night, Storm's lightweight rug had slipped and he now had a large stable stain on his near flank.

"Oh, why have I got a grey horse!" Amy groaned.

She fetched some water and a grooming kit, then set to work on cleaning him up.

As soon as he was looking respectable again, Amy started on the stalls. She finished Dylan's in double-quick time, then grabbed the wheelbarrow handles and began to take the dirty straw up to the muck heap, half-running to save time.

Just before she got there, the barrow wheel hit a stone. Amy lost her grip on the handles and the load toppled to one side, spilling dirty straw and droppings all over the yard.

"Oh, great!" Amy shouted in frustration.

"Having fun?"

Amy swung round.

Ben Stillman, one of Heartland's stable-hands and Amy's friend, was grinning at her. She'd been so busy she hadn't heard him arrive. "You know, most people wait until they get to the muck heap before they tip the wheelbarrow, Amy," he commented, an amused look on his face.

"Not funny!" Amy exclaimed.

Luckily, Ben realized that she didn't need teasing that morning. "Hey, come on," he said easily, "I'll help you clear up."

He fetched a broom and started to sweep up the dirty straw. "Having a bad morning?" he said.

"You could say that," Amy said despairingly. "I still haven't braided Storm yet. I overslept."

"It's not surprising, the hours you've been putting in recently," Ben commented. "Calm down. I'll braid Storm for you after I've done Red."

"Thanks, Ben," Amy said, feeling a weight drop off her shoulders. "You're a star."

"I know," Ben said with a grin. He put the brush away and they went back down the yard together. "You know, I'm sure Ty wouldn't mind doing the extra stalls on a show morning," he said as they walked down to the front stable block with its white-painted doors and hanging baskets full of flowers. "Why don't you ask him?"

A smile lifted the corners of Amy's lips as she thought about Ty, Heartland's main stable-hand and her boyfriend. "He's already offered," she told Ben, "but I feel bad enough going off to shows and leaving him to work all the horses without getting him to do my share of the stalls too." She shrugged. "I can cope."

"If you don't oversleep," Ben said dryly.

"Yes — if," Amy said with a grin.

By seven o'clock, she had finished four stalls and was sweeping up in front of them. When she saw Ty's pick-up turning into the driveway, Amy's heart turned in her chest. Since they'd started dating a few months ago they'd had their ups and downs, but things were going really well between them now. Ty helped Amy treat the horses at Heartland while Lou, Amy's older sister, managed the business side of things and Jack, the girls' grandfather, helped out by doing maintenance on the farm and running the house.

"Hi there," Ty said, getting out and coming over. He glanced around at the tidy yard. "You seem very organized," he said, looking impressed.

"You should have seen it an hour ago," Amy grinned. "Organized was not the word for it then. But Ben's been helping me. I've mucked out four of the stalls in the front block and done all the waters."

"Great," Ty said, kissing her. "I'll go and do the feeds."

While Ty gave the horses their breakfast feeds, Amy gave out the hay nets, finished the two remaining stalls in the front block and then loaded her show gear into Ben's smart black trailer. Finally, she led Storm into the trailer beside Red. "I can't believe it's only eight o'clock," she said, as she and Ben got into the pick-up. "It already feels like the middle of the day." She sank back into the seat and looked out of the window as Ben started the engine. She had a whole hour now doing nothing while Ben drove them to the show. Bliss!

But even though her body was able to relax, her mind couldn't. She kept thinking about Heartland and all the horses who needed working. Luckily both she and Ben were in early classes. They should be back in time to help Ty in the afternoon. They were so busy at Heartland. Amy's best friend, Soraya, usually helped out, but she was away at camp for the rest of the summer. And having a great time, if her e-mails were anything to go by!

Amy ran through the horses in her mind. There was Dylan, the clumsy young showjumper in the stall next to Storm's. Then there was Solitaire, a headstrong yearling who was at Heartland to learn some manners. They both needed working that day. And then there was Willow, the new pony, who was terrified of people; they hadn't even started working her yet. And Sundance, Amy's pony. He was recovering from a tendon strain and would soon need some light riding. There was lots for her to do.

"You're quiet," Ben said, interrupting her thoughts.

"I'm just thinking about everything there is to do back home," Amy told him.

"Well, don't," Ben said firmly. "Right now you should be thinking about the show – and Storm."

"I know. It's just that..." Amy's voice trailed off. It was difficult to explain. She loved taking Storm to shows, loved the buzz, the excitement. But it wasn't easy leaving Heartland behind. There were so many horses there who needed her love and attention. She glanced at Ben. He wouldn't understand. He liked working at Heartland but it wasn't his passion – he lived for jumping his horse, Red. "It doesn't matter," she said quietly.

"So, thoughts firmly on the show then?" Ben ordered.

"Yes," Amy smiled, pushing Heartland out of her mind, "thoughts firmly on the show."

* * *

By the time they arrived, the competition was already well under way. Horses were being warmed up and grooms hurried about, brushes in hand.

While Ben went to the secretary's tent to book in and collect their numbers, Amy saddled up Storm. Her class – the Junior Jumpers – was scheduled to start shortly in the second jumper ring.

"Here," Ben said, coming back and handing her number. "They seem to be running on time. They said you should be able to walk the course in about ten minutes."

"Great," Amy said, gathering up her reins. "I'll go and start working him in."

She found a quiet spot behind the trailers. She liked to just have time with Storm on his own before she took him into one of the busy practice rings.

As she rode round on a loose rein, Amy felt herself relaxing. Storm was a joy to ride. Sensitive and well-schooled, he obeyed her lightest aid. Most of the horses at Heartland had come from upsetting circumstances and demanded every ounce of brain power and concentration that Amy had, but Storm had never been treated badly. She patted his neck. He was one of the lucky ones.

"Amy!" It was Ben calling her. "Time to walk the course!"

Ben held Storm while Amy went into the ring. The brightly painted fences looked solid and big – they were just under four feet high – but Amy didn't feel nervous. Storm could jump them easily. She walked up to each fence, working out where she should steady Storm and where she should push him on. It was a timed first-round class, which meant that the horses who jumped clear continued straight on without a break to jump a shortened course against the clock.

As Amy reached the second-to-last jump, a big red wall, she stopped. On the other side of the wall a slim girl with long blonde hair was assessing the distance to the last jump. It was Ashley Grant. Amy drew in a breath.

Ashley's mother, Val Grant, owned a highly successful hunter-jumper barn called Green Briar where she used harsh training methods to produce push-button horses and ponies. Ashley had a showjumper called Bright Magic. He hadn't been responding to Val's methods and, a few weeks ago, Ashley had secretly asked Amy for help. Amy had agreed but she had been left feeling betrayed and used when Ashley had turned her back on her advice and returned to riding as her mom liked.

Amy didn't want to speak to Ashley and she was about to walk past without a word when Ashley turned.

"Amy!" she said and her cheeks flushed slightly.

Just for a moment, Ashley seemed to hesitate, but then her eyes hardened into their usual cool expression. "I can't see why you're looking at this jump, Amy," she said. "It's not as if you're going to get this far around the course."

"Sorry?" Amy said, raising her eyebrows. She folded her

arms. "Just a reminder, Ashley, but I did happen to beat you last time."

"Fluke," Ashley said coldly.

"Really?" Amy said in disbelief. "Well, let's see what happens in the ring today then."

A strident voice rang out. "Ashley!"

Val Grant was standing by the ring entrance, frowning. "Hurry up!" she shouted to Ashley. "Magic needs warming up!"

"See you when I ride into the ring to collect the blue ribbon," Ashley said, as she marched away across the ring.

"What was Ashley saying to you?" Ben said when Amy returned to him and Storm.

"Just her usual dumb comments," Amy said, shaking her head. "I can't believe I helped her with Magic! I really thought she wanted to change, but she's just the same as ever."

"It can't be easy having a mom like hers," Ben said slowly.

Amy looked across to where Val Grant was giving Ashley a pep talk. "They're welcome to each other," she said.

"Forget about the Grants." Ben touched her arm. "You should be concentrating on Storm — and those jumps in there."

"You're right." Pushing all thoughts of the Grants out of her mind, Amy mounted and rode Storm into the warm-up ring.

Val Grant was walking towards one of the practice jumps.

She was shouting at her daughter, who was now mounted on Bright Magic.

"Use your crop! Take hold of his mouth! Show him you mean business!"

Amy took Storm down to the other end of the ring and worked him until he was really listening to her, then she turned him towards the practice fence. Val Grant was still standing next to it, one hand idly slapping a crop against her leather riding boots. Storm saw the crop rise and fall, and spooked slightly as he approached the jump, taking off too close and catching the pole with his front legs.

He shot off after the jump, shaking his head.

"He's going to have to jump cleaner than that in the ring, Amy," Val Grant called as she put the pole back up. "He could be a good horse if you got after him and taught him a lesson or two."

"Like I'm going to take advice from you," Amy muttered under her breath as she struggled to bring Storm back under control. Slowing him to a trot she circled him until she felt him relax. Seeing the jump was free, she made her canter circle bigger and popped him cleanly over it with no fuss.

Val Grant nodded unsmilingly.

Patting Storm, Amy slowed him to a walk. There were four horses before her. She'd let him have a short rest now.

As she walked him round outside the practice ring she kept one eye on the ring. Ashley was called in on Bright Magic. Amy halted Storm and watched. How would Magic jump? He'd been looking quite agitated in the practice ring. Working with him and Ashley, Amy had quickly realized that the horse was very sensitive. When he was ridden quietly, he jumped well, but if he was pushed and pressured, he tended to panic. She had got Ashley riding him in a snaffle bridle without a crop and he had been jumping beautifully, but at the last show Ashley had listened to her mom and had hit him. He had panicked and jumped badly. Amy watched curiously. How would Ashley ride him today?

To her relief, she saw Ashley loosen the reins of her double bridle as soon as she was away from her mom. Bright Magic lowered his head slightly and seemed to relax. As the starting bell went, Ashley fumbled with her crop. It fell to the ground, but Ashley didn't stop to get it. Stroking Magic's neck, she headed him towards the first jump, a smile flickering across her face.

*She's done it on purpose*, Amy thought. *She meant to drop it*.

Calm now that the crop had gone, Magic jumped the first fence perfectly.

"Good," Amy breathed. She caught herself. She was competing against Magic – she shouldn't be willing him on! But deep down she knew that she cared about Magic's happiness more than the competition. She'd rather see him happy, and herself get beaten by Ashley, than see him stressed.

Ashley and Magic jumped both the course and the jump-off course clear and rode out to the sound of applause. As Ashley left the ring, she passed Amy.

Amy hesitated but then, remembering the way Ashley had dropped the crop, decided to be civil. "Good round, Ashley," she called.

"Thanks," Ashley said briefly without slowing. She rode over to her mom.

Val Grant, all smiles now, congratulated Ashley. Seeing Amy watching, she smiled smugly. "You're going to have to go some way to beat that, young lady," she called out. "Isn't she, Ashley?"

Ashley nodded, avoiding Amy's eyes.

Amy turned Storm away. "Just watch me try," she muttered. Setting her chin, she gathered up her reins. "Come on, Storm," she whispered, "let's show everyone what we can do."

Amy cantered Storm into the ring. She had never felt as determined to beat anyone in her life as she felt to beat Ashley now. Seeming to sense her determination, Storm's ears pricked. The starting bell rang out and then they were away. Jump after jump flowed beneath them. They finished the first part of the course and Amy heard the bell ring indicating that she should continue.

She touched Storm's neck with her fingertips. "Let's go for it," she whispered as they passed the timing post.

Storm flew round the course, cutting corners and turning inside the jumps. As they cantered through the finish to the sound of applause, Amy listened for the loudspeaker. It crackled into life.

"A great double clear there for Amy Fleming on Summer Storm," the announcer said.

Amy looked at the clock and inwardly punched the air. She'd done it! She'd beaten Ashley by more than three seconds.

Ben was waiting outside the ring. "You were on fire!" he exclaimed. "What got into you?"

"Just something Val Grant said," Amy told him.

Ben grinned. "In that case you should pay her to say something to you before you go in every class. No one's going to beat that time!"

He was right. Of the twenty horses that followed, none of them beat Storm.

Grinning with delight, Amy rode Storm into the ring to collect the blue ribbon.

Ashley was in second place. As the judge moved down the line, giving out the ribbons, Amy wondered if Ashley would congratulate her but Ashley stared resolutely ahead. Feeling irritated, Amy couldn't resist making a comment.

"Magic went well in the ring, Ashley," she said. "You must be really pleased. *How* did you get him going so well?"

"You know how I did it," Ashley said abruptly.

"I guess your mom doesn't, though, does she?" Amy shook her head. "Why don't you just say something to her, Ashley? You can't just keep just keep dropping your whip in each class. She *will* notice, you know."

Ashley frowned at her. "It's not that easy."

As Amy saw Ashley's tense face, she remembered Ben's words and felt strangely sorry for the other girl. He was right. It couldn't be easy having Val Grant as your mom. "It's OK," she said, more quietly. "I understand."

Ashley stared at her. "What do you mean, you understand?" The judge looked back curiously in their direction. Ashley immediately lowered her voice. "You don't know anything, Amy!" she hissed.

Amy was stung. "I know it can't be easy living and working with a mom like yours."

"You leave my mom out of this!" Ashley whispered furiously.

"Calm down!" Amy said, shrugging. "I was just trying to say I felt sorry for you."

Two bright-pink spots of colour stained Ashley's cheeks. "You! Feel sorry for me? When my family have got Green Briar and all you've got is your rundown little barn with its two muddy training rings and its scrapyard horses." Haughty pride filled her green eyes. "Get real, Amy. Save your sympathy for yourself. I don't need it!"

Just then the steward came back up the line. "Time for your lap of honour," he said cheerfully to Amy. "Off you go."

Amy's cheeks blazed as she pushed Storm into a canter. *That is definitely the last time I try to help Ashley!* she thought. *She and her mom deserve one another!*

Ben was clapping as she rode out. He stopped when he saw her furious face. "What's up with you?" he said in surprise.

"Just two words: Ashley Grant," Amy said through gritted teeth.

Sensing her tension, Storm threw his head up anxiously. She took a deep breath. "It's OK," she said, patting him, "I'm not angry with you."

Just then Nick Halliwell came over to them.

Amy smiled in surprise and thoughts of Ashley left her mind.

Nick Halliwell was a showjumper whom Amy had first met a year ago when she had helped cure one of his young horses of its fear of trailers. Since then Nick had sent several of his horses to Heartland. They were helping one of his horses – Dylan – at the moment.

"Congratulations, Amy. You jumped a great round," Nick said, "I was watching in the stands. Your horse can certainly jump," he said, patting Storm's neck.

Amy smiled, glowing at the praise.

"Where did you get him from?" Nick asked.

"My dad bought him for me when he was over here on business. He looks for young sports horses to export to Australia and found Storm in Florida."

"Maybe I should ask your father to find one for me," Nick said. "I could use a horse like him." He nodded at Ben. "How's Red going?"

"Good – I hope," Ben replied. "My class is next." He looked at the ring where they'd just finished raising the jumps for the Intermediate. "I'd better walk the course," he said to Amy. "Catch up with you at the trailer."

"Sure," Amy replied

As Ben left, Nick turned to Amy. "So, how's Dylan?"

"Good," Amy replied. Dylan had come to Heartland because of his poor coordination and lack of balance. She and Ty had put in a lot of work getting him to go through a grid of poles on the ground and his coordination was gradually starting to improve. "We've been working him with trotting poles and he's starting to come together. He should be ready to come home soon."

"Good," Nick nodded.

Someone shouted Nick's name. "Look, I've got to go," he said to Amy. "But I'll come and visit soon." He patted Storm. "Take good care of this horse – he's very talented."

He walked off. Feeling delighted at his praise, Amy dismounted and began to walk back to the trailer. She was almost there when she saw her friend Daniel hurrying across the grass in front of her. She called across to him and he stopped.

"Hi," he said, he grinned, pushing his brown hair out of his eyes and coming over.

"I didn't know you were here today," Amy said.

She had first met Daniel when he had been competing on the circuit. At that stage he had been hoping to get a place as a working pupil at a showjumping barn, but when he lost his horse, Amber, in a tragic accident, he had needed a job. He had taken up a stable-hand post at Green Briar a month ago.

"I've been helping a client who's been riding in the Amateur-Owner in ring one," Daniel told her. "How are you? Have you been in the ring yet?"

Amy nodded. "In Junior Jumpers. We won."

Daniel grinned. "How did Ashley do?"

"Second," Amy replied, unable to suppress a triumphant smile.

Daniel raised his eyebrows. "Guess the Grants won't be pleased about that."

Amy grinned. "No."

He looked at his watch. "I'm due a break. Have you got time to chat?"

"Sure," Amy said. "How about we buy a couple of drinks and take them back to the trailer?"

"Sounds great," Daniel replied.

They sat on the ramp of the trailer and drank their Cokes while Storm grazed at the end of his lead-rope. "So how's it going at Green Briar?" Amy asked.

"Not great," Daniel admitted. "At first I guess I was just glad to have a job. I needed something to stop me thinking about Amber…"

Amy looked at him sympathetically. She knew how hard it was to lose a horse, especially a horse as special as Amber. "But now?"

Daniel hesitated. "I don't know. I thought I wanted a job with no commitment, no emotional involvement, but, well —"

he shrugged — "to be honest, I'm hating it. To me horses aren't goods to be bought as cheaply as possible and then sold for the highest price."

Amy nodded. "It must be hard."

Daniel nodded. "It's Mrs Grant's impatience that gets to me," he went on. "Everything has to be done as quickly as possible. There's this horse she bought two weeks ago. He's a great type, he's won a load in equitation but he's been off work for a year since his rider went to college. She's got him back into full-time work already. His muscles should be being built up gradually but she wants to sell him before the season ends." He sighed. "I find things like that difficult to deal with."

"So what are you going to do?" Amy asked him curiously.

"Don't know," Daniel replied, shrugging again. "Look for another job, I guess."

"Have you thought about looking for a working-pupil place again?" Amy said.

"I'm always looking but there's nothing going." He changed the subject. "So, come on, tell me about you. How's everyone at Heartland?"

Amy filled him in on all the news.

As he listened to her talk, Daniel started to look thoughtful. "You know, you might be able to help me," he said. "There's a young horse at Green Briar — a boarder who's come to be broken in — he's really withdrawn and quiet. His owner told me his stable companion — an old hunter — died a few months ago and I think he might still be grieving for him. Do you know of anything I can give him that might help?"

"You could try Bach Flower Remedies," Amy answered. "But without seeing the horse it's hard to say which one you should use. There are several that are useful for grief."

"Maybe you could come and take a look at him?" Daniel asked. "And tell me which one to use."

Amy laughed. "Yeah, Val Grant would really love that! Me on her yard treating her horses. I don't think so."

"She's at a show all day tomorrow with some clients," Daniel said. "You could come then. Please, Amy. This horse needs help."

Amy hesitated. She was useless at turning down horses in need. "Well, I guess I could ask Lou to drop me off for twenty minutes or so," she said reluctantly.

"Thanks!" Daniel said in delight. He glanced at his watch. "I better move it," he said, jumping up. "Mrs Grant's bound to have some work lined up for me to do. I'll see you tomorrow then."

"I'll call you if I can't make it," Amy said. "Otherwise I'll come about ten."

"See you then," Daniel said.

When it was time for Ben to go in his class, Amy went to watch. "You be good," she told the big chestnut horse as Ben tightened his girth after warming up. "Good luck," she said to Ben.

Ben cantered into the ring. Amy watched anxiously but Red was on top form and he managed a double clear with a fast time.

"Looks like it's Heartland's day," Ben grinned as he trotted out of the ring, patting Red hard.

He was right. No one else managed to beat his time and when they drove out of the showground at lunchtime, there were two blue ribbons displayed on the dashboard and both Amy and Ben had prize-money cheques in their pockets.

Amy looked at the two rosettes. "Why can't every show be like this one?" she said, sighing happily.

"It can," Ben said. "We're the dream team!"

Amy grinned. "The dream team indeed."

Looking out of the window, she rode Storm's round again in her mind. It had felt amazing – almost as if they were flying. She thought about her next show, in two weeks' time. She couldn't wait to capture that feeling again.

The countryside rolled by and at last they arrived back at Heartland. As Ben parked the trailer outside the farmhouse, Lou, Amy's older sister, came hurrying down the yard.

Amy jumped out of the pick-up and waved the ribbons. "Hey, Lou! We did really well," she said. "Storm and Red both won their classes and…" She rummaged in her pocket and produced the cheque she had won. "This is for Heartland."

Lou glanced at the cheque. "That's good," she said, distractedly.

Amy frowned. "What's up?"

Lou ran a hand through her short blonde hair. "It's Sundance," she said. "He's sick. I think he's got colic."

# Chapter Two

"Colic!" Amy exclaimed.

"I called Scott," Lou said, looking worried. "He came round and gave Sundance an anti-spasmodic injection."

"I'll unload Storm, Amy," Ben said quickly. "You go."

Amy ran up the yard. She felt sick at the thought of Sundance being in pain.

She reached the barn. Ty was standing in Sundance's stall. The buckskin pony was moving from one leg to the other restlessly. Seeing Amy, he lifted his head and whickered.

"How is he?" Amy asked, going into the stall.

"Slightly better," Ty replied. "The injection Scott gave him seems to be kicking in."

Sundance pushed his nose into Amy's chest. Amy rubbed his golden ears and he sighed deeply as if relieved that she was finally with him.

"How did it happen?" she asked Ty.

"There doesn't seem to be any obvious reason," Ty replied. "About half an hour after you'd gone, I noticed that he was looking restless and when he started trying to roll and kick at his stomach I called Scott. We couldn't find anything that might have started it off. Scott thinks it's just one of those things." He put an arm round her shoulders.

Amy felt a wave of guilt as the pony nuzzled her. Sundance had needed her and she'd been at a show. "I should have been here," she said.

"You were only gone for half a day," Ty said reasonably. "It could just as easily have happened when you were at school or out shopping or something." He shook his head. "Don't beat yourself up over it. It happened. We coped."

Amy stroked Sundance and didn't say anything. Logically she knew Ty was right but somehow it felt worse knowing that she had been at a show enjoying herself.

"Look, why don't you stay here with him for a while," Ty said. "I'll get on with the work – with this happening, we've got way behind. Lou and your grandpa have been great; they've done all the mucking out, but none of the horses have been worked yet. If you stay with Sundance, I can get started."

Amy nodded. "Thanks, Ty."

"No problem," he said.

Amy kissed Sundance's forehead and started to move her fingers in small circles on his neck. It was a form of therapy called T-touch that they used a lot at Heartland. As she gently pushed his skin over his muscles, she breathed deeply and shut her eyes. If only she hadn't gone to the show. *Still*, she told herself as her fingers worked over Sundance's neck, *at least I'm here now – that's all that matters*.

Half an hour later, Sundance's head hung low and his eyes closed. He looked relaxed and calm, and Amy crept from the stall. He needed to rest.

She made her way down the yard. Storm was looking over his half-door. Ben had taken his travelling boots off and brushed him over, but he still had his braids in. He nuzzled Amy in a puzzled sort of way. Amy understood. Normally when she got in from a show, she spent time brushing him over, unbraiding him and massaging his legs. He must have been wondering where she was.

Just then Lou came out of the tack-room. She was carrying some scissors and a small stool. "There you are. I was just going to unbraid him for you."

Amy smiled gratefully. "Thanks, Lou." She reached for the scissors and stool. "I can do it. Sundance is resting now."

"I don't mind if you want to get on with riding the other horses," Lou said. "I know everything's got really behind today."

Amy knew she should take Lou's offer of help but she didn't want to just go off and leave Storm. He'd been so good at the show. She hesitated, feeling torn.

"I really don't mind," Lou insisted.

"OK, thanks," Amy said, forcing a smile. "I'll go and find Ty and see what needs doing."

Ty was riding Dylan round the ring on a loose rein. Seeing Amy walking to the gate, he rode Dylan over. "How's the patient?"

"Resting," Amy said. "Who do you want me to work?"

"Well, I'm just about done with Dylan and Ben's coming in here next to school Major. You could start work with Willow if you think she's ready to do anything."

Amy looked at the next-door paddock where Willow, a bright-bay pony of about fourteen hands, was grazing.

Willow had been traumatized by a bad experience with an old-fashioned horse-breaker. The breaker had taken the young bay pony straight off the fields, tied her to a post and hit her with sacks to try and crush her spirit. Willow, a nervous pony anyway, was now completely terrified of people and her new owner had sent her to Heartland to see if they could help her regain her confidence.

Amy walked over to Willow's paddock. She didn't really have a plan of what to do but sometimes she found that that was the best way of working with a difficult horse. Going in with a set plan could stop you listening to what the horse really needed.

She opened the gate. Willow had trotted to the bottom of the field at her approach. Amy watched her for a moment and then walked into the field. She had no rope and she made no sudden movements but just the very sight of her approaching made Willow throw her head up in fear. With a snort, she took off around the paddock, her head angled to the outside of the field.

Shoulders rounded, head down, Amy stood very still. At first, Willow cantered blindly, but, as the minutes passed, she began to slow down. She still didn't dare to glance in Amy's direction but after a few more circuits she slowed to a halt. She stood for a moment and then wheeled round and set off in the opposite direction.

Amy didn't move. Willow kept on cantering but, after a few more circuits, it was clear she was starting to tire. Dark patches of sweat were appearing on her back and she was breathing quickly. She slowed to a trot. As soon as she did so, Amy had an idea and took a few steps backwards. She wanted Willow to realize that she wasn't trying to hurt her, that she could slow down and Amy wouldn't try to catch her. Willow trotted another circuit before slowing to a walk. Amy quickly stepped back another few steps. As if realizing what was going on, Willow halted and turned to look at her for the first time.

To reward the pony, Amy backed slowly out of the ring.

Ben was riding Major in the school. Seeing Amy leave Willow's field, he rode over. "Doesn't she want to join-up with you?" he said.

Join-up was another technique they used a lot at Heartland. It was a way of communicating with the horse and getting its trust. But Amy hadn't been trying to do that with Willow. "I wasn't trying to get her to join-up with me," she told Ben. "All I wanted was for her to look at me."

She saw him frown in confusion.

"When you join-up with a horse you have to use aggressive body language to chase the horse away from you," Amy explained. "Willow's much too frightened to be able to cope with someone doing that just now. If I'd tried it I'd have made her even more scared."

Ben shook his head. "You know, I could work here for ten years and I still wouldn't be able to figure the needs of each different horse like you," he said. "How do you do it?"

Amy shrugged. "It just comes to me." She paused, wondering whether to say more, but Ben looked genuinely interested so she decided to elaborate. "I didn't always know what to do." She hesitated. "At first, after Mom died, I felt really helpless. Whenever I worked with a horse I just kept wondering what would she have done. But then I gradually started to trust my own instincts. Now I just seem to know what's needed. Not all the time, of course," she qualified, "but more than I used to."

"You and Ty are something else," Ben said. "I'll never have your instincts."

"Well, you've got other talents," Amy told him, knowing it was useless to pretend otherwise. "You can stay on anything. Major would have had me off five times already if I'd been working with him. You haven't fallen off him once."

Ben grinned. "Superglue on the saddle. You should try it."

They exchanged smiles. Amy patted Major. "Well, I'd better get moving," she said. "See you down on the yard."

The rest of the day raced by. Amy worked with Willow twice more — each time simply standing in the middle of the field and waiting until the pony felt brave enough to look at her and then rewarding her bravery by backing away and leaving. On the third time, it only took the little bay a few minutes of cantering round before she stopped and looked at Amy. She still showed no signs of coming anywhere near her, but there seemed to be a new curiosity in her eyes, as if she was starting to think about what Amy was doing rather than just blindly running away. Amy was satisfied. The progress Willow was making might be slow but at least it was progress.

By the time the last hay net had been put into the last stall, at six o'clock, Amy was wiped out from her long day. It seemed a long time since she had got up that morning. She waved off Ty and Ben, and then went wearily to Storm's stall. He pushed her affectionately with his nose. Amy sighed. She knew she should spend some time with him.

"I'm sorry, Storm," she told him, stroking his nose, "but I'm beat."

He nuzzled her, not understanding. Amy rested her forehead against his face, feeling torn. She was just so tired. Her stomach growled ravenously.

"Tomorrow," she told him, and, having given him a last kiss, she walked down to the house.

# Chapter Three

"I'll come back for you in half an hour," Lou said as she dropped Amy off in the parking lot at Green Briar the next morning.

Amy nodded. "Thanks." Half expecting someone to stop her and demand to know what she was doing, she walked towards the barns. All three training rings had horses working in them, and in the jumping ring she could see a beautiful steel-grey Trakhener just completing a course of four-foot fences. The rider drew him to a halt, then swung her leg over the saddle, dismounted and handed the reins to a stable-hand who was waiting at the gate. "Here. I'm done," she said and, without so much as patting the horse, strode from the ring.

"Amy!"

Amy looked round and saw Daniel hurrying towards her.

"Thanks for coming," he said, jogging up to her. "Come and meet Midnight – the horse I told you about."

Amy followed him across the yard. It was immaculate. Hardly a strand of straw littered the floor and all the yard brushes and mucking-out tools were stacked neatly. Daniel walked into the nearest barn and stopped at the door to the second stall. A black colt with a white blaze was standing quietly in one corner, his head down, his muzzle almost resting on his straw bed.

"That's all he does," Daniel said. "He just stands there like that."

Amy went into the stall. The colt didn't even look up. "You said his stable companion died?" she said.

"Yes," Daniel replied. "It was the owner's old hunter. Midnight had been kept with it ever since he was weaned."

Amy stroked the colt's black coat. "What happens when you turn him out?"

"He grazes but he's very withdrawn," Daniel said.

"And what about feeding?" Amy asked, her eyes not leaving the subdued colt.

"He eats OK," Daniel replied. "He likes his food."

Amy thought for a moment. "Give him the Honeysuckle Bach Flower Remedy," she said at last. "It's the best remedy for loss. If Midnight was so uninterested in life that he wouldn't eat, Wild Rose or Olive might work better, but I think Honeysuckle is the one you need. Add ten drops to his water each day and maybe give him ten drops of Walnut as well – it will help him adjust to the change in his surroundings."

"Thanks," Daniel said. "I hate seeing him so low."

Amy patted the colt. "You'll get better soon, Midnight."

They left the stall. "So how are you feeling about yesterday?" Daniel asked. "Have you come back down to earth yet?" He saw her blank expression. "The show. Winning the Juniors…"

Realization dawned on Amy's face. "Oh, that."

Daniel shook his head. "Amy! Most people wouldn't be able to think of anything else for at least a week!"

"I know, and I'm pleased," she said. "It's just that there's a lot on right now at Heartland." She tried to explain. "I never seem to have time for everything. There are so many horses that need our help at the moment."

"It must be tough," Daniel said sympathetically.

Amy nodded. Although she kept trying to convince herself she could cope, it was getting harder to fit in shows as well as doing all her work at Heartland. The last few days had proved that, what with Sundance getting colic while she was at the show. She sighed inwardly. She always seemed to feel guilty about something lately.

They walked out on to the yard. A handsome dark-bay horse of about sixteen hands was tied up to a nearby hitching rail. A stable-hand was standing beside his shoulder, while another stood by him with a raised broom.

Amy frowned. "What's happening there?" she asked Daniel.

"Duke's been playing up when he has his feet picked out," Daniel replied. "I told you about him – he's the horse that's won quite a lot but has been off work for a year."

"Oh yeah," Amy said remembering. "The one who Val's got back in full-time work already."

Daniel nodded. "He was great until a few days ago but then when the farrier came he just freaked. Ever since then, he hasn't wanted his feet touched."

"Maybe the farrier pricked him with a nail," Amy said.

"He didn't get as far as actually putting shoes on," Daniel replied. "Duke blew up as soon as he tried to put his hoof on the stand. Val reckons he's just playing up but he doesn't strike me as an awkward kind of horse."

Amy watched as the stable-hand near Duke's shoulder reached down to pick up the horse's hoof. The second he touched Duke's leg, the horse flung himself backwards.

"Stop that!" the stable-hand behind him shouted, smacking him with the broom.

Amy flinched. She saw the fear in the horse's eyes. "He's scared," she said quickly to Daniel.

The first stable-hand was reaching for Duke's leg again. This time the horse's ears went back even before the stable-hand had touched him, he half-reared but once again the broom smacked into him. Duke threw his head up, his eyes showing the whites. "Stand up!" the stable-hand shouted, hitting him again.

"Daniel! Please stop them!" Amy said urgently.

Daniel stepped forward. "Hey, you guys." The stable-hands looked round. "Why don't you give Duke a break? He looks quite stressed. Maybe you should let him cool off a while."

"We're just doing what we're told. Mrs Grant said he's got to learn," one of the boys replied. He waved the broom behind Duke, making the horse shoot forward.

Amy couldn't hold herself back any longer. "But can't you see he's frightened? Look at him!"

The stable-hand looked at Daniel. "Who's your girlfriend?"

Before Amy could tell him, Daniel stepped forward. "She's just a friend," he said, putting a warning hand on her arm. Immediately she realized that he didn't want them to know she was from Heartland. "Look, guys, leave Duke. He's a good horse. He doesn't deserve this. I'll speak to Mrs Grant about him."

To Amy's relief, the stable-hand shrugged and put the broom down. "Well, if that's what you want."

Daniel pulled Amy's arm. "Come on."

"Idiots," Amy muttered under her breath as she walked away.

"They're only following instructions," Daniel said. "Mrs Grant believes that all horses should be forced to learn respect."

Amy shook her head. "I don't know how you can stand to work here."

Daniel shrugged. "It's a job."

Amy looked at him. "You don't mean that."

For a moment Daniel didn't reply, and then he sighed. "No, I don't," he admitted. "I hate it."

"So get another job," Amy told him.

"If only," Daniel said. "I don't have a reference from my last job because I left so suddenly, and the Grants aren't likely to give me one if I leave here so soon. No decent yards will look at me without references."

Amy saw the despondency on his face. "Something will come up," she said hopefully. "I'm sure it will." She glanced at her watch. "I'd better go. Lou will be here any minute."

As she spoke, Ashley came round the corner. She was wearing skin-tight cream breeches and a Giorgio Armani T-shirt. "Amy!" the word burst from her in surprise. "What are you doing here?"

"I…" Amy didn't know what to say.

"She just stopped by to say hi to me," Daniel said quickly.

Ashley turned on him, her eyes narrowing. "Shouldn't you be working?"

"I'm on a break," he replied curtly.

"Well, when you're off it, I'd like Magic saddled up," Ashley ordered.

"Never heard of the word 'please', Ashley?" Amy said, raising her eyebrows.

Ashley swung round to look at her. "Listen, I don't like you and you don't like me, Amy," she snapped, "so why don't you just stay away from my family's yard?"

"With pleasure," Amy retorted. She glanced at Daniel. "I'll call you."

"OK, see you," he replied.

Amy marched away. To her relief, Lou was just drawing into the car park. Amy opened the car door and jumped in. "Get me out of here fast," she said with feeling.

Lou glanced at the yard and grinned. "Let me guess – Ashley Grant?"

"Got it in one," Amy replied.

When Amy got back to Heartland, she helped Ben and Ty finish the stalls, then she went up to Willow's paddock. She worked the pony just as she had done the day before, letting her run and then rewarding her for stopping.

The fifth time she entered the paddock, Willow merely trotted round several times before halting. She looked at Amy and then lowered her head. There was a new softness in her expression – a certain curiosity. Amy took a small step backwards and paused. Willow hesitated and then took one hesitant step towards her.

"Good girl," Amy whispered. She left the paddock, her spirits high.

She went to Storm's stall. He had been out in the field and she was relieved to see that the swelling in his legs from his hard work the day before had just about gone down. "I'll give you a groom," she said, "and then I'll rub in some Black Pepper and Eucalyptus oils – that should make any stiffness go away."

She fetched her grooming kit and the diluted oils and set to work. Storm seemed to love the attention. As she massaged the warming oil into his legs he snorted happily. He was such an affectionate horse, it made her feel doubly bad when she was too busy to spend time with him.

Amy straightened up after doing his two front legs, rested her head against his warm neck and breathed in his sweet smell. "I love you," she told him.

"Amy!"

She went to the door. Ty was looking for her. "Can you help me with the lunchtime feeds?"

Amy's heart sank. She hadn't finished Storm yet. But what could she do? "OK," she called back resignedly.

She patted the grey gelding. "I'll be back soon," she promised.

But after she'd helped feed she had to help Ty bring some more hay from the main barn to the small hay-store off the feed-room and then they had to sweep up. In the end it was almost an hour before she got back to Storm's stall.

Feeling the tension mounting inside her at the thought of everything she had to do, she unbolted Storm's door. "Hi, Storm, I'm back."

He nuzzled her in greeting.

She had just picked up a bottle of oil when she heard Ben calling her name.

She looked over the door. "Can you give me a hand bringing some of the horses in?" he asked.

*No!* Amy felt like shouting but she knew she couldn't. Taking a deep breath, she put down the oil and left Storm's stall. "Fine," she said.

Ben heard the tension in her voice. "What's up?" he asked in surprise.

"Nothing," she replied abruptly. "Come on."

Storm put his head over the door and whinnied in surprise as she walked away. Amy felt awful. *Still*, she told herself, *all I've got to do is help bring the ponies in and then I can get back to him.* "I'll get Solly," she told Ben.

Ben nodded and haltered Jigsaw and Jasmine.

Solitaire, a headstrong yearling who was at Heartland to learn some basic stable manners, was at the side of the field watching curiously as Grandpa fixed a bar in the fence that had come loose.

*Please be good*, Amy thought.

As soon as the chestnut foal saw the other two ponies being led out of the field, he came trotting over to the gate.

"Here, Solly," Amy called.

To her relief, Solitaire walked straight up to her.

"Good boy," Amy praised as she buckled up his halter. She opened the gate and the foal immediately barged forward, trying to catch up with Jigsaw and Ivy.

"No!" Amy said, stopping him. "You mustn't pull!"

Turning the foal in a circle, she led him back into the field and started to walk down the yard again. Solitaire walked three paces and then raced forward after the ponies.

"Solly! Stop that!" Amy said.

Feeling her frustration mounting, she turned Solitaire back to the gate. "You are not going down to the barn if you pull like that," she told him. "Just walk nicely!"

The foal looked after Jigsaw and Ivy and whinnied loudly. It was clear he wanted to be with them.

"Come on," Amy pleaded with him. "I haven't got time for this." She clicked her tongue. Solitaire walked beside her for ten paces. Amy was just breathing a sigh of relief when suddenly the little foal barged forward, his shoulder almost knocking Amy over.

"Solitaire!" Amy exclaimed, pulling the foal up sharply. "Stop it!" Solitaire half-reared. As he came down, one of his front hooves landed squarely on Amy's foot.

"Ow!" Amy cried. Pain and anger blinded her and her hand flew up. "You stupid…"

She stopped on the very point of smacking Solitaire's neck. The world seemed to stand very still for a moment and then slowly she lowered her arm. She breathed out shakily. What was she thinking of? She'd almost hit a horse!

"Amy?" She swung round. Grandpa had dropped his fence tools and was hurrying across the field towards her, a look of concern on his face. "What's going on?"

# Chapter Four

Amy stared at Solitaire with horrified eyes. Completely oblivious to the situation, the chestnut foal pulled impatiently in the direction of the barn.

"Amy," Grandpa reached them. "What's the matter?"

"I ... I almost hit him," Amy said, her face pale with shock.

"You're just tired — you overreacted," Grandpa said, putting a comforting hand on her arm. "Here. Take a few moments out. I'll take Solitaire."

Amy started to hand him the lead-rope, but then she stopped. "No. I have to do this," she said. Taking a deep breath, she touched the foal's neck. "Come on, Solly," she said, forcing her voice to sound calm and controlled. "Back to the gate."

She led the foal back up the path. Inside she was still reeling from the shock of what she had almost done, but she was determined she was going to get Solitaire to lead without losing her temper.

It took three more attempts but finally Solly seemed to get the message that barging would only result in him being taken back to the gate. On the fourth time, he walked quietly beside Amy all the way down to the barn. Amy took his halter off.

"See, it wasn't so difficult after all," she said, patting him. She spoke cheerfully but inside she was very aware of Grandpa watching her, his eyes furrowed in concern.

"Amy," he said, as she tried to hurry past him with the halter. "Are you OK?"

Amy stopped. "I think so."

"Let's go down to the house," Grandpa said quietly. "We should talk. I'm worried about you."

Her heart thudding, Amy followed him down the yard.

They went into the kitchen. Amy hovered by the doorway.

"What's going on, Amy?" Grandpa asked softly. "I've never known you lose your temper with a horse."

Amy rubbed her forehead with one hand. "I was just feeling stressed, I guess."

Grandpa sighed. "You have been working very long hours."

"I can cope," Amy said quickly.

"Can you?" Grandpa fixed her with his blue eyes. He took her hands in his. "It doesn't strike me that you're very happy at the moment." He shook his head. "You've got so much going on in your life. Look, how about you ease up on your workload with the horses? We could get some temporary help in."

Amy stared at him in shock. Cut back on working with the horses? "No," she said quickly. "I couldn't do that."

"Well, maybe you should think again about competing Storm," Grandpa suggested. "Maybe you haven't got time for that as well as everything else."

"But I love the shows," Amy protested. She shook her head. "No. I'll be fine, Grandpa. Really I will."

He looked doubtful.

Just then the kitchen door opened and Lou came in from the office. She took in the tension on Amy's face. "What's wrong?"

"Amy and I are trying to work out a way to make her life a bit less hectic," Grandpa replied.

Lou frowned in concern. "You have been working really hard lately," she said to Amy. "Maybe I could help more," she offered. "Now I've got the advertising all set up, I've got more time on my hands. I could groom Storm for you each day and clean his tack if it would help." She shot Amy a quick smile. "Just don't ask me to ride him."

Amy half smiled. A few weeks back, Lou had tried to ride Storm but it had been a disaster. Having only just started riding again after thirteen years out of the saddle, Lou had been far too unsubtle with her leg and hand aids for a sensitive, highly schooled horse like Storm.

"I could do other things, too," Lou continued. "I don't

know enough to work the difficult horses but I could ride some of the quieter ponies, like Jasmine and Jigsaw, who just need taking out on the trails. Just let me do things for you."

"Thanks, Lou," Amy said.

"I'd be happy to do your share of the stalls on show days," Grandpa said.

"I'd appreciate that," Amy said.

He smiled. "We're both here for you, Amy. We both want to help you any way we can."

"Thanks," Amy said. But she knew there wasn't any more they could do. It was working with the problem horses that took up most of her time and that was one job that she couldn't hand over to anyone else even if she wanted to. She stood up. "I'd better get on," she said. "I'll see you both later."

They nodded and she hurried out of the kitchen.

Over the next few days, Lou started grooming Storm and cleaning his tack. It saved Amy some time but she found she really missed spending time in his stall with him. Several times, Amy caught herself thinking back over Grandpa's words and wondering whether she really could keep on going as she was. It was hard enough now but what would happen when she went back to school in a few weeks' time? But she knew she would never cut back on working with the horses. So what was she going to do? *Nothing*, she decided, pushing her concerns to the back of her mind. *I'll just carry on as things are. I'll cope.*

On Thursday morning, Daniel rang Amy. "Hi," he said. "I thought I'd just ring and give you an update on Midnight."

"How is he?" Amy asked, remembering the black colt.

"Doing well," Daniel replied. "I added the remedies to his water on Monday and he's been like a different horse. He's stopped standing in the corner all the time and he's taking more of an interest in things."

"That's great," Amy said, feeling pleased that she'd been able to help.

"So, how have you been?" Daniel asked her.

"Busy," Amy answered. "How about you? Seen any new jobs yet?"

"No," Daniel answered. "And Mrs Grant's driving me crazy. Do you remember Duke? The horse who wouldn't have his feet picked up?"

As if she could forget. "Yes, I remember him," Amy answered.

"Well now she's got handlers standing behind him with a crop, hitting him every time he moves back. The horse is totally freaked out. He used to be really good in the stable but now you can't get near him. He's constantly got his ears back and he's always threatening to bite or kick."

An image of the handsome bay gelding came into Amy's mind. He'd had such a wise face, it was awful to think of him becoming so confused and scared that he had taken to kicking. "Can't you do anything?" But even as she spoke she knew what the answer would be. Val Grant ruled Green

Briar with a rod of iron and she wouldn't stand for any of her lowly stable-hands telling her what she should or shouldn't be doing.

"Like what?" Daniel said. "I got into enough trouble after stopping Jed and Kevin that time you visited. Mrs Grant has put me on a formal warning. If I step out of line again I lose my job." He sighed in frustration. "I just wish she could see that what she's doing is going to ruin Duke."

Amy heard the unhappiness in his voice. "Look, why don't you come and visit us here?" she suggested. "When's your next day off?"

"Sunday," Daniel replied.

"Well come over," Amy said. "You haven't seen Ty or Grandpa or Lou for ages. I'm sure they'd really like to catch up with you."

"All right," Daniel said, sounding more cheerful. "I'd love to come over. I'll come round about nine, if that's OK."

"Great," Amy said. "Do you want to stay for brunch as well?"

"I'd love to," Daniel said. "Thanks. I'll see you Sunday then."

After Amy replaced the receiver, she sat down at the table. She couldn't stop thinking about Duke. She hated the thought of him becoming aggressive. She chewed on a fingernail. If only there was something she could do. But Val Grant was hardly likely to listen to her and if Daniel said anything he'd get sacked and then he wouldn't have a job or anywhere to live and that wouldn't help Duke.

Amy sighed and stood up. Well, there were horses outside that she *could* help. She'd better go and get started with them.

Willow was grazing in the field. As Amy opened the gate, the pony looked up sharply but didn't run away and Amy felt a glow of satisfaction. Every moment she was spending with Willow was paying off.

She walked to the centre of the field. Willow moved away but, whereas she had once cantered blindly, too scared to even look in Amy's direction, she now simply trotted, her eyes flicking towards Amy every few paces. Amy stood still. After two circuits, Willow lowered her head and slowed to a halt.

Amy stepped backwards. Willow took a step towards her. To reward her bravery, Amy walked back another pace. Willow stared at her intently. Acting on instinct, Amy turned away and crouched down near the ground. There was a long pause and then she heard Willow starting to walk towards her across the paddock

Amy's heart beat fast but she forced herself to stay still. This was the first time Willow had taken more than just a step or two towards her. She could hear Willow's hooves on the grass. The pony was close now, almost close enough to touch. Amy felt the air move as Willow reached down and then her nose brushed against Amy's shoulders.

Amy counted to three and then, moving very slowly, she

turned. Willow stared down at her, her dark eyes wide and watchful. Reaching up, Amy touched her neck.

Willow tensed for a moment and then a long sigh left her. Not daring to stand up in case she frightened her, Amy gently rubbed her neck.

Willow lowered her head and started grazing by Amy's feet. Amy waited for five minutes, until the pony had moved a couple of feet away, and then slowly straightened up. Willow raised her head anxiously.

"It's OK," Amy whispered, not wanting to push too much in one day. "I'm going now." She started to back towards the gate. Willow hesitated and then came after her. Amy's heart leapt. Willow was choosing to be with her, she wanted to join-up and be friends.

When she reached the gate, Amy stopped and stroked the pony's shoulder. Willow's skin twitched but she stood quietly, her eyes on Amy's face, full of trust. Amy smiled in delight. A breakthrough had been made.

Over the next two days, Amy spent as much time with Willow as she could. With each session Willow's confidence seemed to grow. By Saturday night, Amy could pat her all over.

"You're doing really well, Willow," Amy praised as she led the pony around the paddock.

Willow suddenly tensed and looked in the direction of the gate. Amy glanced round. Ty was there. "It's OK," Amy said softly. "Ty won't hurt you."

Willow was still very nervous around people other than Amy. She stared anxiously in Ty's direction, her muscles tensed. To show that she was listening to her and that she understood her fear, Amy unbuckled the halter and set her free. "See," she said, "I won't make you go near Ty if you don't want to."

She patted Willow, then walked over to the gate.

"How is she?" Ty asked.

"Good," Amy replied. She glanced round. Willow was following her. The pony stopped about nine feet away from the gate but the fact that she had come so close to Ty was a huge improvement. "She's getting braver every day."

"I'm going home now, Amy," Ty said. "Everything's done on the yard. Are you finished?"

"Not yet, I'm going to ride Storm," Amy said, leaving the paddock and starting to walk down the yard with him.

Ty looked at her ruefully. "I guess it's no use asking if you want to go out and catch a movie then?"

Amy was torn. She really wanted to say yes, but if she went to a movie then she wouldn't have time to ride Storm and she had a big show coming up in just a week's time – her first time ever competing in the High Junior Jumper class.

"Hey, don't stress about it," Ty said, seeming to see her confusion. "It's OK, I know the horses come first."

He spoke understandingly but Amy felt bad. They were supposed to be dating but she never went out anywhere with him. Still, when did she have the time?

"See you, then," Ty said and, putting his hands on her shoulders, he kissed her.

Amy shut her eyes. Being in his arms felt so right.

"See you…" she whispered, as they eventually parted.

"Tomorrow," Ty said, completing her sentence with a smile.

That night a strong wind blew up and, when Amy went outside to feed the horses the following morning, there was loose straw from the muck heap blowing all over the yard.

"Oh, great," Amy muttered, looking round at the mess. Cleaning it up was going to take some time.

Ignoring the whinnies of the horses in the front stable block, eager for their breakfast, she hurried up the yard to check on the paddocks. During the summer months, most of the ponies at Heartland lived out day and night, and Amy was worried that the wind might have damaged some of the fences or brought a tree down.

But, to her relief, all seemed calm in the paddocks. The fences appeared intact, if a little battered, and Jigsaw, Ivy, Solitaire, Jasmine, Sugarfoot and Blackjack were all grazing happily, their manes and tails blowing in the wind.

Willow was the only pony not grazing. She was pacing around her paddock, her head held high, her eyes tense and worried. Amy climbed over the gate. The little bay gave a relieved whicker and trotted over. "It's OK, girl," Amy told her as the pony stopped and nudged her anxiously with her nose. The wind often made even calm horses jumpy and flighty and Willow was looking wound up.

Amy gently smoothed the pony's forelock. "There's nothing to get worked up about," she told her. "It's just the wind." Gradually Willow relaxed.

"I'm going to have to go and feed," Amy said, after ten minutes. "But you'll be all right. Look at the other ponies — they're not worried."

Willow snorted and, after giving her a last pat, Amy left the field.

By the time Daniel arrived at nine o'clock the wind had dropped slightly and Willow seemed more settled. After saying hi to everyone, Daniel went with Amy to Storm's stall. "How's he going?" he asked her.

"Good," Amy said, stroking the gelding's nose.

"He sure looks well," Daniel said. Lou had already groomed Storm that morning and the dark-grey dapples on his snowy-white coat gleamed.

"Do you want to ride him?" Amy offered.

"Can I?" Daniel said eagerly. "Will he be OK in the wind?"

Amy nodded. "He's a real honey, nothing ever seems to upset him."

She tacked up Storm and led him up to the training ring. Just as Amy had predicted, Storm ignored the wind and did everything she asked for, walking, trotting and cantering at the slightest aid.

When Storm was warmed up, she rode him over to the gate then dismounted and held the reins out to Daniel. "OK," she said. "Now you have a go."

Daniel fastened his hard hat and mounted. At first he simply walked and trotted Storm round on a loose rein while they got used to each other but then he started asking the gelding to work a little harder, getting Storm to collect and work through transitions and lateral work.

Amy watched, fascinated. She'd never really seen Storm being ridden before. Daniel rode lightly, like she did, and Storm went very well.

"I'll put a jump up for you," she called, after ten minutes.

She dragged a jump into the middle of the ring, then set the bar at just over three foot.

Daniel cantered him round and popped Storm over it.

"Shall I raise the bar?" Amy called.

"Sure," Daniel said, patting Storm.

Amy raised the jump to three foot six. When Storm cleared that, she raised it again to just over four foot. Once again, he jumped it perfectly, powering upwards from his hocks and clearing it with room to spare.

Daniel rode over to Amy, his eyes were shining. "Incredible!" he said. "It's like he could jump anything."

Amy nodded, delighted to have someone else to share her appreciation of Storm. "He's brilliant," she enthused.

Daniel looked at the fence. "Do you want to put it higher?"

"Sure," Amy said. As she raised the pole, she glanced at Daniel. He was circling Storm in a trot, his lips moving as he spoke quietly to the gelding. He turned Storm towards the fence. Storm's ears pricked. He found his stride perfectly, rising through the air and clearing the fence with inches to spare.

Patting him hard, Daniel slowed him to a trot. "You are so lucky," he said, riding up to Amy, his eyes glowing. "Storm's the best."

"I know," Amy said, with a smile.

Just then an empty paper feed-sack blew up the yard and smacked into the gate. Storm jumped slightly at the sudden flapping noise.

"It's OK, boy," Amy told him quickly, and, feeling her hand on his neck, he relaxed.

"Amy!" Daniel said quickly. "The pony in the next-door field. Look!"

Already hearing the sound of hooves, Amy swung round. Willow was galloping round her paddock, her ears pinned back.

"It's the feed-sack!" Amy gasped. She ran across the ring chasing after the sack. The sound of it crackling and rustling was clearly reminding Willow of her experience with the horse-breaker. Amy grabbed it and crumpled it into a ball but Willow was too terrified to notice that the noise had stopped. Head high, eyes full of panic, she was galloping straight towards the fence.

# Chapter Five

"No!" Amy whispered in horror as Willow approached the fence. What would she do? Would she try and jump? She'd never clear it. The pony's muscles tensed but the fence was high and at the last minute she swerved. Her hooves slipped on the short grass, and she fell.

"Ty!" Amy shouted in alarm. She scrambled over the training ring fence. "Ty! Ben! Come quick!"

Dumping the offending sack into a nearby water-butt, she raced into Willow's paddock. The pony was already struggling to her feet, dust and loose strands of grass falling from her sides.

"Hush, girl," Amy soothed, slowing to a walk so as not to risk alarming her. To her relief she saw that Willow seemed to be bearing weight on all her legs. *Please don't be badly injured*, Amy prayed.

Willow whickered as she saw her. When she reached her, Amy put her hand on the pony's warm neck. "There now," she soothed. "Everything's going to be OK."

Willow pushed her head against Amy's chest and breathed out heavily as if to say, "I'm safe now. You're here."

Amy's eyes raked the pony's body for injuries. There were a few minor cuts but that seemed to be all. Hearing voices at the gate, she glanced round. Ty and Ben had heard her shouts and came running up the yard. Daniel seemed to be explaining to them what had happened,

The next minute, Ty came hurrying across the field.

Hearing his footsteps, Willow threw her head up nervously. Ty stopped. "Is she OK?" he called anxiously.

"I think so," Amy replied, starting to check the pony over.

"Daniel said she just took off round the field," Ty said.

"A feed-sack blew against the gate," Amy explained. "She panicked at the sound – it must have reminded her of the horse-breaker." She stroked the filly's face. "I'd better stay with her. Can you ask Daniel to put Storm away for me?"

"Sure," Ty said. "Call me if you need me."

Twenty minutes later, Willow had calmed down enough for Amy to lead her down to a stall. To her relief, the young pony seemed to have nothing more wrong with her than a few bumps and bruises.

Ty was filling a water bucket on the yard. "How is she?"

"Quieter," Amy replied. "She doesn't seem to have hurt

herself but I think I'll add some Rescue Remedy to her water to help her get over the shock of it all. Where's Daniel?"

"With Storm," Ty said.

Amy went to find them. Daniel had unsaddled Storm and was standing with the gelding, his fingers moving over Storm's face in the same light T-touch circles that Amy always used. They both looked so peaceful.

"Hey there," Amy whispered.

Daniel looked up and smiled.

Amy let herself into the stall. "Thanks for bringing him in for me."

"No problem. How's the pony?"

"Calmer now," Amy said. She looked at Storm's contented expression. "He seems to be enjoying himself."

"He's a special horse," Daniel said warmly.

"But a special horse who doesn't get enough attention, do you, boy?" Amy said, stroking Storm's shoulder.

"It must be tough, trying to compete him and do everything here," Daniel said.

"It is," Amy said. She looked at Storm. "Lou's been grooming him for me and cleaning his tack but it's still difficult to get time to ride him, let alone take him to shows. I'm always needed with the other horses and he has to come last."

"Look, if I can help at all, just say," Daniel said. "If you need a hand exercising him, I could come here after work."

Amy shook her head. "Thanks, but it wouldn't work. It's weird enough having Lou grooming him for me. If you were exercising him as well then I'd never spend any time with him. I'd just be getting on him at shows and that would be wrong."

"I understand," Daniel said. "But the offer's there if you want it."

Thanks," Amy said.

"Amy — are you there?"

Hearing Lou's voice, Amy looked out over the door. "I've got Nick Halliwell on the phone," Lou called from the house. "He wants to call in to see Dylan in about half an hour. Can I tell him that's OK?"

"Sure," Amy called. She turned back to Daniel. "I'd better go groom him before Nick gets here."

"I'll give you a hand," Daniel said.

Forty minutes later, Nick Halliwell's Lexus turned into the yard. Dylan, the big clumsy bay, whickered when he saw his owner. Nick stroked him. "He's looking good," he said to Amy, his eyes taking in Dylan's shining coat and muscled neck and hindquarters.

"He's really improving," Amy said. "I'll take him out in the ring so you can see."

Daniel helped her fetch Dylan's tack.

"So, how's that lovely showjumper of yours?" Nick asked when Amy came back.

"Pretty good," Amy said with a smile.

"Jumping out of his skin," Daniel said, swinging the saddle on to Dylan's broad back.

Amy caught Nick looking at Daniel curiously and realized she hadn't introduced them. "Nick, this is Daniel Lawson," she said. "He's a friend of mine. Daniel, this is Nick Halliwell."

"Pleased to meet you," Nick said holding out his hand. As Daniel shook it, he frowned. "I don't know you from somewhere do I? You look familiar."

"We've jumped together a few times," Daniel said. "We were both in the Six Bar at the Meadowville show."

Nick nodded. "Of course! I remember now. You ride that roan mare – unusual-looking but a great jumper. I haven't seen you on the circuit recently. How she's going?"

The air in the stall suddenly seemed to freeze. Amy hardly dared look at Daniel.

"She, er…" Daniel cleared his throat. "She was put down last month. She broke a leg."

Confusion and embarrassment washed over Nick's face. "I should have remembered. Amy did tell me at the time. I'm really sorry. How stupid of me!"

"It's OK," Daniel said quietly.

There was an awkward pause.

"So, what are you doing with yourself now, Daniel?" Nick asked, breaking the silence. "Did you ever find that working-pupil place you were looking for?"

Daniel shook his head. "I'm working as a stable-hand – at Green Briar."

"For the Grants?" Nick raised his eyebrows. "How are you finding it?"

"Not great," Daniel admitted, tightening Dylan's girth. "I'm actually thinking about moving on."

"Got a job in mind?" Nick asked.

Daniel shook his head. "I guess I'll just take whatever comes up."

Nick looked thoughtfully at him and then patted Dylan. "OK," he said to Amy. "Let's get this fellow working."

As Amy rode Dylan round the ring on a loose rein to warm him up, she watched Nick and Daniel chatting by the gate. She was pleased they seemed to be getting on well. Daniel could sometimes be reserved and defensive with people he didn't know well, but he seemed to be talking to Nick OK.

Feeling Dylan start to relax, she concentrated on him. Collecting the reins, she began to walk him over a grid of six poles she had laid out on the ground earlier. The idea was that, instead of simply riding the horse over them as you would do with traditional trotting poles, the poles were also used as a maze. If the horse was asked to walk round the poles instead of over them, he had to bend his body first to the right and then to the left and really concentrate on what he was doing. It was part of a training system called T-team developed by a horsewoman called Linda Tellington-Jones. T-touch was part of the same system.

As Dylan walked out of the maze of poles on the other

58

side, Nick called out to her. "Why are you making him do that?"

"It's to help him become more aware of his body," Amy explained, riding Dylan over to the gate. "He has to really concentrate on where he is going and that helps improve his general coordination and balance."

"He certainly looks more confident and less clumsy," Nick said.

"He is," Amy replied. "I'll show you what he's like on the flat in a few more minutes."

She took Dylan through the maze several times and then, when she was sure he was feeling relaxed and confident, she rode him away from the poles and asked him to trot on. Keeping him on a fairly short rein she rode him through a series of transitions, circles and serpentines. Whereas once Dylan would have found the more collected work difficult, he now accomplished what she asked easily.

"That's a really big improvement," Nick said, looking impressed as she finally halted Dylan at the gate.

Daniel nodded. "I remember seeing him when he first came here – I was staying here for a while – he was so clumsy then."

"He's really coming on," Amy agreed, patting him. "He should be ready to come back to you soon, Nick."

Nick nodded. "That will be good. We can start jumping him then." He looked doubtful. "Though I'm not sure he's ever going to make a successful showjumper. It's a pity. I bred him myself from one of my top mares."

Amy nodded. She too had her doubts about Dylan's future as a showjumper. Dylan was a lovely horse and his coordination was really improving but top-level show-jumpers needed superb balance and coordination. "He's very long in the back, isn't he?" she said, knowing that such a characteristic wasn't ideal in a showjumper. "And, although he's improving, I don't think his coordination is ever going to be perfect."

To her surprise, Daniel spoke up. "I think you're being too hasty. He's only a baby at the moment. I know he looks long now but sometimes big warmblood horses like him just take a few extra years to grow into their bodies. With the correct work he should muscle up and his body shape will change and as that happens his natural balance should come. He's got great hindquarters for a showjumper – really sloping – and his hocks are good and powerful. I wouldn't give up on him yet."

Amy looked at Nick, wondering how he'd take Daniel's comments. One of the things she liked about Daniel was that he wasn't awed by people and spoke his mind openly regardless of who he was talking to, but sometimes people who didn't know him took offence at his direct attitude. However, to her relief, she saw that Nick didn't look offended. He was looking at Daniel with interest.

"It's strange you should say that," he said. "Dylan's dam did exactly the same. She didn't have Dylan's coordination problems but she was a big gangly youngster. It was only when she hit seven that she seemed to mature and then she really started to perform. She turned into one of the best mares I've ever had. Not quite a top-class Grand Prix horse but a brilliant puissance jumper." He looked at Dylan. "Maybe you're right, maybe he does just need time."

"It's impossible to tell," Daniel said. "But if I were you, I wouldn't give up on him just yet."

Their eyes met and Nick smiled. "I might just take that advice, Daniel. Thank you. It's good to meet someone who speaks their mind." He turned to Amy. "Can I have a ride round on Dylan? See what he feels like?"

"Sure," Amy said, dismounting.

As Nick rode Dylan round the ring, she joined Daniel at the gate.

"Nick's a really nice guy, isn't he?" Daniel said. "I've never really talked to him before. But he seems really genuine — not like some showjumpers."

"He is," Amy said, watching as Nick skilfully rode Dylan around the ring. "And he really cares about his horses."

"I like him," Daniel said.

Nick left after riding Dylan. He was very pleased with the young horse's progress and agreed to visit again the following week to set a day when Dylan should return to his yard.

Daniel stayed on for brunch and then helped out with the horses. At the end of the afternoon, Amy walked with him to his pick-up.

"You take care now," he said to her. "Don't work too hard. When's your next show?"

"Next weekend," she replied. "It's at East Creek. I'm going in the High Junior Jumpers – it'll be our first time in the higher division."

"Storm will hardly even notice the height difference," Daniel said, climbing into his truck. "He's one hell of a horse, Amy."

"I know," Amy smiled

"Well, good luck," he said, starting the engine. "I'll give you a call soon."

That night, Tim Fleming, the girls' father, phoned. He lived in Australia. For twelve years he had been out of Amy and Lou's lives but then, six months ago, Lou had traced him. She and Amy were now in regular contact with him.

"So, how's Storm going?" he asked Amy.

"Great," Amy enthused. "We won again at the weekend."

"Junior Jumpers?"

"Yep. The low division, but we're going in the higher division for the first time next Saturday."

"Excellent," Tim said. Amy could hear the smile in his voice. "Soon you'll be competing in Intermediate and Open."

"I wish," Amy said.

"What's all this *I wish* business?" her dad said. "You've got the talent. You're going to make it into the big time with Storm, Amy. I can see it now. World Championships, Pan-Am Games..."

"Dad!" Amy said, laughing. "Get real."

"You've got the right horse for it," her dad said. "If you want it enough, you'll make it happen."

Amy didn't say anything. *If you want it enough…*

The question was, how much *did* she want success with Storm? Enough to make it her one aim in life? Enough to give up her work at Heartland?

"Amy?" her dad said.

"Yeah, I'm still here," she told him.

"Listen, if you need anything for Storm, just let me know," he said. "I know how expensive competing can be. Soon you'll be wanting to travel further to shows and as he moves up the grades you'll be having to stay at places for days at a time. It'll cost money but I'm more than happy to fund you – I'd like to help."

"Thanks," Amy said. She wished that it was just a question of money, but it was much, much more. She thought for a moment about talking to her dad about her Heartland showjumping dilemma but, the instant the thought had formed, she knew there was no point. When he was younger, his life had been totally focused on showjumping. He'd never understand how she could want to do both.

"Is there something wrong?" Tim asked as the silence went on.

"No," Amy said quickly. "No, nothing's wrong. So … so, how are you, Dad? How's business going, and how're Helena and Lily?"

They started to chat about Tim's work and about his new wife, Helena, and their baby daughter.

When Amy finally replaced the receiver, she stood for a while in the silence of the kitchen. Sometimes she felt like she was being torn in two. She knew how much her dad wanted her to succeed with Storm – and she wanted that as well, but then there was Heartland.

She walked to the window and looked out. Jake, Dancer and Storm were dozing over their stable doors, their heads nodding, their eyes half-closed. It was such a peaceful scene that Amy felt a warm rush of pride. Her mom had made Heartland what it was and now she and Ty were carrying the work on.

But what about her showjumping dreams? If she was going to make it to the top then she was going to have to start travelling with Storm. She would have to leave Heartland for days at a time to compete in shows in other states.

Her heart clenched and in an instant she knew that she couldn't do it. She couldn't leave Heartland and the horses that needed her. *I belong here*, she thought.

But if she didn't travel then she and Storm could never get beyond a certain level on the show circuit. She would be stuck in the lower divisions, forced to watch while people like Ashley moved on and up. Amy knew she wouldn't be able to bear that either.

"What do I do?" she whispered, looking out at the quiet yard.

No answer came.

# Chapter Six

Over the next few days, Amy hardly had time to think about the future. Her patience and work with Willow seemed to be paying off. The pony didn't seem to be suffering from any after-effects from her fall, and by Wednesday she was happily letting Amy tie her up, groom her and put a rug on and off.

As Amy eased the rug off Willow's back and watched the little pony standing quietly, she felt a warm glow of happiness. To see a pony who had once been so terrified now starting to trust and look calm made all the time she had spent seem worthwhile.

"She's doing great."

Amy turned and saw Ty watching, a little way off.

"She is, isn't she?" Amy smiled, knowing Ty would share her satisfaction. Putting the rug down quietly, she moved to the pony's head and untied her. "Why don't you try coming closer?" she suggested. "She might be all right now."

Amy massaged Willow's neck with T-touch circles. Ty walked slowly closer, his eyes lowered, his body language as unthreatening as possible. Amy could see Willow watching him but the pony didn't try to move away. As Ty reached Amy's side, Willow lifted her head slightly. "It's OK, girl," Amy murmured.

Ty stood quietly and Willow gradually started to relax again. All the time Amy's fingers worked on Willow's neck. Seeing the wariness leave her eyes, Amy had an idea.

"Put your hand on mine," she said softly to Ty.

Ty didn't need to ask why. He placed his fingers lightly over hers. Willow tensed slightly but as Amy massaged her, she relaxed again.

Amy could feel the warmth from Ty's palm dissolving into the skin on the back of her hand. She closed her eyes, her breathing matching Ty's as their fingers moved together on Willow's neck. The world around them seemed to disappear until there was nothing left but the two of them and the little bay pony they were working on.

She didn't know how long they stood there, but little by little the world slipped slowly back into her consciousness and she opened her eyes. She looked up and met Ty's eyes. Then, without speaking, she moved her fingers out from under his so that he alone was touching Willow. She stepped quietly back. The pony watched her but allowed

Ty to keep on moving her skin with his strong, sensitive fingers.

Delight swept through Amy — Willow was finally accepting someone else's touch, and it was something that she and Ty had done together.

After a few minutes, Ty patted Willow and stepped back. His eyes met Amy's and she stepped forward and impulsively kissed him. "Thank you," she said to him, feeling totally happy.

Ty smiled warmly. "Any time."

All day, Amy glowed with the buzz she had got from working Willow with Ty. *There really is nothing like working with damaged horses*, she thought as she rode Storm down the yard that afternoon. *Not even jumping in the ring.*

She thought back to the warmth she had felt as Ty's hand had moved with hers. Suddenly she heard the phone ringing. A moment later, the back door opened and Lou looked out.

"Amy, Daniel's on the phone. Here, I'll take Storm for you," Lou took the reins and, having dismounted, Amy went into the house.

"Daniel, how are you?" she said, picking up the phone.

"Fabulous!"

Hearing the excitement in Daniel's voice, Amy said quickly, "What's up?"

"I have just had the best day ever!" Daniel said.

"Why? What's happened?" Amy demanded.

"Nick Halliwell rang me this morning and, you'll never guess what, but he's offered me a job! As a working pupil!"

"A working-pupil place! Daniel, that's great!" Amy exclaimed.

"I've been to visit his yard this afternoon," Daniel went on. "It's amazing — top-class horses, nice people, and Nick … well, he's great. I watched him working a range of horses from a green four-year-old through to Brave Knight, his Grand Prix jumper. I'm going to learn so much from him. I can hardly believe it!"

Amy was delighted. "It's wonderful! You'll have a great time. Nick's fantastic."

"I know." Daniel's voice dropped. "I … I just wish Amber could be going with me."

There was a pause. Amy didn't know what to say.

Daniel sighed, "I always used to dream that one day I'd get a working-pupil place and that Amber and I would make it to the top together. Now my dream's starting to come true, only it's without her. It's a different dream."

Amy hesitated. "Dreams change," she said quietly. "They have to."

"Yeah — I guess they do," Daniel said quietly. She heard him take a breath and then he changed the subject. "I can't wait to leave Green Briar."

"When do you start at Nick's?" Amy asked.

"I'm moving there tomorrow," Daniel replied. "I start work on Friday."

"Wow!" Amy said in astonishment. "That's quick. Doesn't Val want you to work your notice?"

"No."

Amy heard a note of hesitation in Daniel's voice and had a feeling that he wasn't telling her something. "Daniel?" she said.

"I ... um ... kind of got myself sacked this evening," he admitted.

"What?" Amy said in astonishment.

"Well, when I got back from Nick's I went to find Mrs Grant to hand in my notice. She was with Duke. She was getting one of the lads to shoot his hindquarters with a pellet gun every time he tried to run backwards when his feet were picked up."

Amy gasped. "What? That's disgusting!"

"He was terrified. I kind of lost my temper and told her that if she didn't stop I'd call the ASPCA. Then I told her what I thought of her and her training methods. She hit the roof and said she wanted me off the yard within twenty-four hours."

"What about Duke?" Amy asked.

"He's totally freaked out. He won't let anyone near him now. She's going to sell him."

"But how will she find anyone to buy him?" Amy said.

"She's just going to send him to a sale," Daniel said. "She'll cut her losses and sell him as unwarranted."

Amy's heart sank. Unwarranted horses usually went for

glue. She thought of the handsome bay gelding. It was such a waste. An idea came to her. "Find out when she's going to sell him," she said quickly. "And let me know."

"Why?" Daniel said. "Are you thinking of buying him?"

"I'll have to talk to Lou," Amy replied, her mind racing. "But we've got the money I won on Storm the other week. So it's a possibility."

"That would be great," Daniel said eagerly. "I'm sure he's not vicious. He was fine when he first came to Green Briar. If you sorted him out you could sell him on and make yourself quite a bit of money."

"That wouldn't be why I'd do it," Amy said.

"I know that," Daniel said. "But he has won a lot, he's well known. You could get a good price for him if he was back on the equitation circuit and going well. Look, I'll try and find out Green Briar's plans for him before I leave tomorrow. I'll give you a ring when I know anything more."

"Thanks," Amy said.

She put the phone down and took a deep breath. Now she had to talk to Lou.

Lou was in Storm's stable, rubbing him down. Amy quickly told her all about Duke and how Val had treated him, about Daniel losing his temper with Val, and finally how Duke was now going to a sale to be sold as unwarranted.

"Poor animal," Lou said, shaking her head in sympathy.

Amy hesitated, wondering how to break her plan to Lou,

but before she could say anything Lou spoke. "We should buy him, Amy," she said quickly. "Then you and Ty could help him here."

Amy stared at her.

"You don't think it's a good idea," Lou said, looking at her uncertainly.

Amy found her tongue. "No! I do, I definitely do," she burst out. "In fact I was about to ask whether we could do just that. I thought we could use the money I won at the show."

"Good idea," Lou said. "It's money we weren't expecting to have so I haven't budgeted to use it for anything in particular. Why not use it for this?" She put down the stable rubber she was using. "Come on, let's go and find Ty and Grandpa, and see what they say."

They hurried across the yard to where Grandpa and Ty were rehanging one of the field gates.

"Hi," Ty said, looking up as they approached.

Seeing them both, Grandpa put down the gate. "Something up?" he asked.

"We need to talk to you about something," Amy said, glancing at Lou. "It's about this horse at Green Briar..."

She told them all about Duke and how he was going to a sale. "I really think we should help him," she finished. "Lou does too."

Lou nodded. "It seems he really needs Heartland. We want to buy him but we thought we'd see what you both thought of the idea."

"I definitely think we should if the accounts can afford it," Ty said immediately. "It sounds like he's had a nightmare time at Green Briar."

"I agree, but what about the time he'll take up?" Grandpa asked, looking slightly worried. "You're being pushed to the limit as it is, Amy."

Ty spoke up. "I'm more than happy to take on the main role of caring for him. I know Amy doesn't have much time at the moment, but I can fit in another horse."

"Thanks, Ty," Amy said gratefully. She looked at Grandpa. "Well? Can we buy him then?"

Grandpa nodded. "Sure. If Lou thinks we've got the money then it's all right by me."

"Thank you!" Amy cried, hugging him. "Thank you so much!"

Amy rang Daniel back and told him the good news.

"That's great," he said. "I've found out that the Grants are planning on sending Duke to a sale next week. But I could always ask her if she'll sell him to me. It would save her the cost of taking him to the sale and paying the ring fee."

"You think she'd let you buy him?" Amy asked.

"I think so," Daniel replied. "She just wants him off the yard and selling him to me will save her money. I'll just tell her I really like him and want to take him with me when I leave."

"How much do you think she'll want for him?" Amy asked.

Daniel named a sum.

"We can afford that," Amy said. "I'll get Lou to get the money out of the bank and we'll meet you in the car park at Green Briar in an hour. Then you buy him from Val and bring him here tomorrow in your trailer."

"OK," Daniel said. "Look, I'll go and speak to her now. If she doesn't agree, I'll call you."

He didn't call, so just under an hour later Amy and Lou drove into the Green Briar car park. Amy looked round anxiously for Daniel. She didn't want to go and look for him in case Val saw her.

A group of children were standing in the nearest training rings. Amy's attention was caught by their smart white breeches and shiny leather boots. They didn't have a mark on them. One by one their horses were led into the ring and they mounted. Without so much as a word to the stable-hands they rode off and formed a neat ride.

Lou shook her head. "Did you see that? None of those four kids thanked the stable-hands. They just took their horses as if they expected to have people running round after them."

Amy remembered the woman she'd seen riding last time she'd visited Green Briar. She too had simply handed her horse over to the stable-hand without a word of thanks.

"I bet they don't even know what a grooming brush looks like," she said. "They just get on when the horse is ready and when they've finished riding they hand it back. I'd hate to do that." She stopped.

A small voice spoke in the back of her mind. *Isn't that what you're doing with Storm? Yesterday Lou untacked him for you.*

"Here's Daniel," Lou said, interrupting her thoughts.

Amy turned. Daniel was hurrying up to the car.

"Here's the money," Lou said passing him the money through the window. "Is everything still all right?"

Daniel nodded. "Mrs Grant's agreed I can buy him. She clearly thinks I'm mad, but just as I thought she jumped at the chance of not having the hassle and expense of taking him to the sale." He looked round. "Look, I'd better go. I'll see you at Heartland in the morning."

Lou smiled. "See you then!"


At nine o'clock the next morning, Daniel arrived with Duke. "He wasn't easy to load," he said. "He doesn't like people too much at the moment."

"I can't say I blame him," Ty said. "I don't think I'd like anyone shooting me in the butt with pellets."

They took the ramp down. Duke kicked out, warning them to stay away.

"He's not really mean," Daniel said. "He's just scared. Where shall I put him?"

"In the front block, next to Jake," Amy said.

Daniel went into the trailer. There was a brief struggle as Duke tried to bite but, handling him expertly, Daniel untied the lead-rope and led the bay gelding out on to the yard. As Duke saw Amy and the others watching him, he pinned his ears back. He looked wary and untrusting.

Amy felt incredibly sorry for him. "Poor thing."

Ty squeezed her shoulder. "We'll get through to him in the end," he said. "I know we will."

Daniel set off to Nick's, promising to ring them in a few days.

"Good luck on Sunday," he told Amy, as he got into his pick-up.

It took Amy a moment to realize what he was talking about. The show! Her first time in High Junior Jumpers. "Thanks," she grinned.

"You'd almost forgotten about it, hadn't you?" Ben said to her as Daniel drove away.

"Yeah," she admitted. "So much has been happening."

"And now you're even busier," Ben said, glancing at Duke's stall. "I don't know how you're going to find time for it all."

"Me neither," Amy admitted. She shrugged. "I guess I'll just have to manage. Come on, let's go and get the ponies in."

Over the next few days Ty spent hours with Duke, while Amy found herself busier than ever. Despite the fact that Willow now tolerated other people handling her, the only person she really trusted was Amy. Amy spent a lot of time trying to build up her confidence.

On Saturday a wind blew up again and Amy decided that it would be safer to stable Willow overnight in case she got upset. She settled the pony in the stall next to Sundance.

"You're going to be OK, girl," she said, massaging Willow's muzzle with dilute lavender oil. The smell of the oil and the touch of Amy's fingers seemed to soothe the pony slightly and she relaxed enough to pull at her hay net.

Amy let herself out of the stall. It was seven o'clock and she still had to get Storm ready for the show. Lou had groomed him but Amy wanted to wash his tail and legs. Quickly she made her way down the yard and fetched some water and shampoo.

He nuzzled her as she came into the stall. Amy kissed his face. She felt like she had hardly seen him properly for days. All she did with him was ride, give him a quick brush over and put him back in his stall or out in the field.

"I'm getting to be like one of those riders at Green Briar, aren't I, Storm?" she said sadly.

Storm rubbed his face against her arm.

His obvious delight at seeing her made Amy feel even more guilty. "I wish I had more time to spend with you. I really do," she told him. "Tomorrow will be different, I promise. It'll be just you and me at the show all day. No one else. Just you and me."

The wind was still blowing strongly when Amy got up the next morning and the first thing she did when she went out on the yard was check on Willow. The little pony was looking jittery. She whinnied when she saw Amy and kicked the stall door.

Amy knew she should really get a move on and start braiding Storm but she couldn't leave Willow in such a nervous state.

She went into the pony's stall and started massaging her lips and muzzle with T-touch circles. Slowly, Willow calmed down and at last Amy felt happy enough to leave her.

Her grandfather was already mucking out the front stable block.

"Thanks," Amy called out as she headed for Storm's stall.

"No problem," Grandpa called back, pressing down the straw in the wheelbarrow. "I hope this wind blows itself out before you get to the show," he said.

"Me too," Amy agreed. "It isn't going to be fun jumping in a wind this strong." She opened Storm's door. "Hey, boy, looking forward to today?"

He snorted and came over for some fuss.

By the time Ben and Ty arrived, Storm was braided and groomed.

"Will you be ready to leave in half an hour?" Ben asked her.

"Should be," Amy replied. She put her grooming kit away, and went to help Ty do the feeds.

\* \* \*

"Willow's looking a bit wound up," Ty said, when he returned to the feed-room with the empty feed buckets a little while later. "She didn't eat any of her breakfast."

Amy looked up from the hay nets. "I was hoping she might have calmed down by now," she said, frowning. "I'll go and massage her with some lavender oil – it worked last night."

"But you've got to finish getting ready for the show. I'll do it," Ty said.

Amy hesitated. She needed to load her stuff into the trailer but she knew that Willow would calm down much quicker for her than for Ty. "Thanks, Ty, but it's probably easier if I do it. She's more likely to relax with me."

He nodded and Amy grabbed the bottle of dilute lavender oil from the feed-room then hurried up to the barn. Willow was pacing round her stall, her ears flickering. Amy poured a little oil into her hand and began to massage Willow's muzzle as she had done the night before. It seemed to work. Gradually Willow quietened down.

"Amy! We should go!" Ben called from the barn door.

"Just five more minutes," she called back, wanting to make sure Willow was fully calm before she left.

"We're running late as it is," Ben said, coming down the aisle. "I've loaded up your stuff but we should get a move on."

Amy hesitated, feeling torn. She really didn't want to leave the pony.

"I'll go and put and Storm in the trailer for you," Ben said.

"It's all right. I'm coming!" Amy said. She kissed Willow's nose. "You be good now, Willow. I'll be back later."

The pony followed her to the door, whickering anxiously.

As Amy hurried towards the barn door she heard Willow whinny after her. She felt a stab of guilt. She shouldn't be going. Willow needed her. She should be staying behind.

# Chapter Seven

"And now in the ring in Class 75, we have Amy Fleming riding Summer Storm," a voice crackled over the loudspeaker.

There was a smattering of applause. Giving Storm a quick pat, Amy trotted him into the ring. *Concentrate*, she told herself. *Focus*.

But it was hard. From the moment she and Ben had left Heartland all she had been able to think about was Willow. Every instinct in her body seemed to be telling her she should be at home.

Storm's hooves barely seemed to touch the short green grass. He looked round eagerly at the brightly painted jumps, the white stands, and he pulled at the bit in excitement.

"Steady now," Amy said. She forced her thoughts on to him. Leaning forward, she let him swing ahead into a canter. The starting bell went.

Turning Storm into the first fence, Amy felt her mind drain clear of everything but Storm and the course of jumps in front of her. All the guilt, the stress she had been feeling, faded into nothingness and she was left with a wonderful feeling of peace. "Come on, boy," she whispered, her eyes fixed on the first fence. "We can do it!"

First lengthening his stride and meeting the jump perfectly, Storm then soared over it. Moving as one with him, Amy guided him skilfully over jump after jump. The grass and crowds were a mere blur, her whole being was focused on the horse beneath her and the jumps they had to clear.

As they landed safely after the last with a clear round, the crowd clapped loudly. Patting Storm's neck hard, Amy rode out of the ring, her eyes shining with excitement and delight.

"He just gets better!" Ben said, meeting her outside the ring.

"He's wonderful!" Amy said, jumping off Storm.

Storm rubbed the side of his face against Amy's chest. She scratched his forehead. "You're the best," she told him.

He snorted and looked around. He looked so happy to be at a show that Amy smiled. "He loves competing."

Ben nodded. "I know you can't see him when he's in the ring but it's like there's a light that goes on inside him when he sees the jumps. I'm sure that's why he's such a brilliant jumper — he just loves being on show."

Ben's mobile phone rang. Looking surprised, he dug it out

of his pocket. "Ben Stillman. Oh, hi, Ty. Yeah, yeah … I'll just get her, she's here."

He handed the phone over to Amy. She took it quickly. Ty! What was he ringing for? All the thoughts that had drained from her mind when she was in the ring suddenly came swarming back.

"Ty," she said in alarm, "what is it?"

"It's Willow," Ty said. "The wind brought down a branch on to the barn roof and the noise has really upset her."

"Do you want me to come back?" Amy asked. She looked at Storm standing so eagerly beside her and her heart sank. She would miss the jump-off and Ben would have to scratch from his class.

"I think you should," Ty said. "She won't let me near her and she's kicking out in her stall. I'm worried she's going to hurt herself."

He didn't have to say any more. "We're coming back straight away," Amy told him.

She saw Ben look at her in surprise. She handed the phone to him. "Talk to Ty."

As Ty explained, Amy looked at Storm. "I'm sorry," she said to him.

To her relief, Ben was in complete agreement with her that they should go back. "There'll be other shows," he said. "You take Storm back and get him ready to travel. I'll speak to the steward and let him know you won't be in the jump-off and I'll scratch Red from his class."

Amy walked Storm back to the trailer. He walked eagerly enough but when she started taking his tack off and getting his travelling boots out he nudged her with his nose in a puzzled way.

"I know, Storm," she said. "You think we should be going in the jump-off, but we've got to go home. I'm really sorry."

For the first time ever, Storm refused to go up the ramp into the trailer. He looked back towards the ring as if he was trying to tell her she'd forgotten something. Amy understood but there was nothing she could do. They had to get back to Heartland.

"Come on, Storm, please," she said, clicking her tongue and trying again.

Storm hesitated and then walked resignedly up the ramp.

Amy thought about Willow all the way home. She never should have left that morning. Her instincts had been right. The second Ben stopped the pick-up, Amy jumped out. There was no sign of Ty – or anyone. She headed for the barn. Reaching it, she heard the sound of hooves kicking wood and raised voices.

"Steady, girl! Steady!"

"Easy there!"

"Shall I call Scott?"

Amy raced down the aisle. She could hear the alarm in Grandpa and Ty's voices. What had happened? She saw Grandpa standing outside Willow's stall. Ty was in the doorway.

"Amy, thank goodness you're here," Grandpa said, seeing her. "Willow's put a back hoof through the wall and it's stuck."

Amy stopped beside Ty and immediately saw what the problem was. In her panic, Willow had kicked so hard at the wooden walls that one of her back hooves had gone straight through the panelling. It was now caught and the pony was trying desperately to pull it free. Her eyes rolled, her ears were flat back and blood from a cut around her fetlock was spattering the wall.

Amy didn't stop to think. "Shush, Willow, easy does it," she said going into the stall.

Seeing Amy, Willow let out a whicker of recognition and stood still.

"It's all right," Amy breathed. Holding out her hand, she stepped closer to the pony. "I'm here. I'll look after you."

Willow's sides trembled. Reaching out with her nose, she touched Amy's hand with her muzzle. Amy stroked the pony's face and neck. "It's OK, girl," she said quickly. "Everything's going to be OK."

Willow pulled at her hoof anxiously.

"Easy now," Amy said. "I'll get you free." She moved slowly round to the wall. Willow's foot had caught behind a piece of wood that had bent down when she kicked the hole and had sprung back when she tried to pull her foot away. Amy held it down. "There, girl."

Willow heaved at her hoof and it came out of the hole. Her fetlock was still bleeding and there was a nasty cut above her hoof but at least she was now free. As Amy moved round to the front of her, she buried her face against Amy's chest and stood there as if trying to hide from the world.

"What happened?" Amy said to Ty.

"I was trying to calm her and she panicked even more," he replied. "That's when she put her foot through the wall."

Amy stroked Willow's hot neck. "I'm glad we got back when we did."

"Me too," said Ty. "There was no way she was letting me near her."

"I've got the first-aid kit here," Grandpa said quietly.

"I'll let her calm down and then we'll see to her cuts," Amy said. "Maybe it would be best if you just left me with her for a while."

They both moved away.

Amy sighed. "Oh, Willow. What are we going to do with you?" She started to massage the pony's forehead with T-touch circles. The pony sighed in relief.

After the pony had calmed down slightly, Amy fetched some water to bathe the cuts on her leg. Ben had unloaded Storm and the gelding was now looking over his stable door. He whinnied eagerly when he saw Amy walking past with the water.

"Sorry, boy," Amy said, "but I've got to look after Willow right now."

As she continued up the yard, Storm whinnied again. Amy stopped and looked back. He was staring at her in confusion. Amy felt awful. He obviously couldn't understand why she seemed to be ignoring him.

She glanced at the bowl of water in her hand. No, she decided, hard though it was, right at this moment, Willow needed her more than he did.

The cuts on the pony's leg were mainly just scrapes and scratches, and none of them were deep enough to need stitches. As she dressed the wounds, Amy kept thinking about Storm — the sound of his whinny, the confusion in his eyes. She felt so guilty. She was being so unfair to Storm, to Willow. *What am I doing?* she thought.

"Um ... Amy," Ty said, coming to the stall door, "do you want me to take Storm's braids out?"

"No ... yes. Oh, I don't know, Ty," Amy cried out, all her suppressed frustration and unhappiness bursting out of her in a sudden rush. She covered her face with her hands.

"Amy? What's wrong?" Ty said quickly.

Amy dug the heels of her fists into her forehead. "I can't do this any longer, Ty," she said in an anguished voice. "I can't be in two places at once." The words came out before she could stop them. "I'm going to stop competing Storm."

As soon as the words left her she wanted to snatch them back, but at the same time, she felt an overpowering feeling of relief. She'd finally said it. Finally admitted that she just couldn't go on as she was doing.

"Hey," Ty said gently, coming into the stall. "It's just been a bad day…"

"No, Ty," Amy interrupted, "it's more than that. I'm being split in two."

"But giving up shows…" Ty's eyes searched her face. "Couldn't you just cut down on the number of shows you do?"

Amy desperately wanted to say yes, to cling to the hope that she could still compete with Storm, but she couldn't fool herself. "It wouldn't work. I'd never be happy. You know me. I'd always be wanting to do more and so would Storm."

Ty didn't argue. He obviously knew she was right. She shook her head. "It's shows or Heartland, Ty. I can't keep doing both. It's not fair on you or the horses or Storm." Her voice faltered as she thought about Storm, about how he would feel never going in a show again.

Just then Ben came into the barn. "How's Willow?" He caught sight of the unhappiness on Amy's face and frowned. "What's up?"

Amy swallowed. Telling Ty that she was giving up shows was one thing – it was almost like talking to herself – but telling Ben made it suddenly public and official. "I…" She forced the words out. "I'm going to give up competing." She waited for his reaction.

Ben stared at her in astonishment. "What did you say?"

Amy felt empty inside. Never to go in the show ring again. Never to fly round a course of jumps like she and Storm had done that day. *It's the only way*, she told herself. She looked Ben in the eye. "I can't do it, Ben," she said. "Not any more. I'm needed here."

She felt Ty's hand squeeze her shoulder in silent support.

"But ... but..." Ben seemed lost for words. "What about Storm?" he said at last. "What will you do with him?"

"Do with him?" Amy frowned. "Nothing. I'll keep him here and just ride him out on the trails."

"But you can't do that!" Ben exclaimed. "He has far too much talent to be wasted that way! You know that."

An image of Storm's happy face at the show came into Amy's mind but she pushed it away. "He'll get used to not competing," she said. She saw that Ben was about to argue more and stood up. "He'll just have to," she said desperately, as she pushed past him.

Storm was looking out over his door. Again he whinnied when he saw her, and she went into his stall and put her arms round his strong warm neck.

He nuzzled her back and tears sprang to her eyes. "I'm sorry, Storm," she whispered. "I really am." Swallowing hard, she stepped back and stroked his handsome face. "You'll be happy," she said. "We might not go to shows but we'll go out on the trails every day. No more schooling. No more boring circles and transitions. You'll like that."

Storm pushed at her with his nose, not understanding, just pleased that she was there.

Amy rested her forehead against his neck. *He'll be fine*, she told herself. *He'll be happy; I know he will*.

# Chapter Eight

"You're not going to go in shows any more?" Lou stared at her. "But why?"

"Because I haven't got time for them," Amy told her.

Grandpa put down the bridle he was mending. "Are you sure about this, Amy?"

"Yes," she said firmly. "I'm giving up competing." It got easier to say each time.

"But what will you do with Storm?" Grandpa said.

"Why does everyone keep asking me that?" Amy demanded. "I'll just keep him for riding on the trails, that's all."

"But, honey, he's been bred to compete," Grandpa said.

"So? What else can I do?" Amy said

Lou glanced at Grandpa.

Amy suddenly didn't want to hear what either of them

might say. "There isn't any other option," she said swiftly. "Storm stays here and becomes a pleasure horse. There's nothing wrong with that. That's all lots of horses do!" Her voice rose defensively.

"It's all right. Don't get upset," Grandpa said quietly.

"I'm not getting upset!" Amy exclaimed. "I just can't see why everyone's making such a big deal about this." She shook her head. "I'm going to my room," she said, and swung round and walked out of the kitchen then up the stairs.

When she reached her bedroom, she sank down on her bed. She *was* doing the right thing. She couldn't keep competing, so Storm would just have to get used to not going in shows. Why was everyone acting like there was some other option. There wasn't, unless ... unless she *sold* him.

The thought had barely formed before Amy was pushing it away. No! Storm was hers. Well, technically he was hers and Lou's, but he was hers in spirit. He loved her. They belonged together. She shut her eyes and saw his handsome face, heard his whinny, imagined him nuzzling her arm. She shook her head. No. She could never part with him. He would just have to get used to his life as a pleasure horse at Heartland. He'd be happy – wouldn't he?

She heard the phone ringing downstairs. A minute later, Lou shouted her.

"Amy! It's Daniel!"

"Coming!" she sighed.

Lou met her on the staircase and handed her the phone.

"Hello," Amy said, going back upstairs. "How's it going at Nick's?"

"Incredible!" Daniel's voice rang with enthusiasm. "I'm riding some amazing horses. Nick likes to designate two or three young horses to all his working pupils and, though I'm supposed to be just a stable-hand at the moment, he's given me charge of two youngsters already. I'm basically in charge of grooming and riding them and, with Nick, I chart their progress and work out their competition schedule for them. It's like having my own horses."

"That's brilliant. And what's everyone on the yard like? Amy asked.

"Really friendly, there's a great team spirit – it couldn't be more different from Green Briar."

"That's good," Amy said.

"So, how's Duke doing?" he asked.

Amy had to think for a moment. "He's OK," she said. "Ty's been working with him. He seems to gradually be realizing we're not going to hurt him."

"And what about the show?" Daniel said. "How was that?"

"Oh, not great," Amy replied. "Storm jumped clear but Ben and I had to leave before the jump-off. Willow had an accident and wouldn't let Ty near her."

"Bummer," Daniel said. "Oh, well, you've got more shows coming up. You're entered for Marriott Park next weekend, aren't you?"

"I was." Amy took a deep breath and broke the news to him. "But I'm not taking Storm in shows any more, Daniel."

"You can't be serious," Daniel said. "But Storm's so talented. You can't keep him out of the ring."

"I haven't got a choice," Amy told him. "I can't keep going to shows *and* run Heartland."

"So get someone else to ride Storm in shows for you," Daniel said.

Amy hesitated. She hadn't considered that possibility. She tried to imagine what it would be like watching Storm go off with someone else to a show, hearing about how he had jumped afterwards.

"How about asking Ben?" Daniel went on. "It would be easy for him to take Storm along to shows with Red."

"No." Amy was already shaking her head. Ben was a brilliant rider but he rode firmly, taking control of horses and making them do what he wanted. His style of riding suited a lot of horses – they took confidence from his strong leadership – but Amy knew it wasn't the right sort of riding for Storm, who liked a very light touch. "He and Storm wouldn't get on together."

"Well, look, how about I ride him for you?" Daniel suggested.

For an instant, a picture of Daniel riding Storm round a show ring flashed into Amy's mind. There was no doubt Storm would enjoy being ridden by Daniel – she only had to think back to how well Storm had gone in the schooling ring for him – but… *No!* The thought filled Amy's mind – clear and definite. And suddenly she admitted the truth. It might be selfish but she simply couldn't bear the thought of Storm going to shows without her – not with Ben, not with Daniel, not with anyone. If Storm was in the ring then she wanted to be the one riding him.

"Well?" Daniel said when she didn't speak.

Amy felt awkward. She didn't want to admit she was being selfish. "Thanks for offering," she said quickly, "but I can't really see it working out, Daniel. You're going to have your hands full at Nick's. Soon you'll be going in shows for him and then you won't have any time to compete Storm."

"I guess that's true," Daniel admitted. He sighed. "I just wish there was something you could do."

Amy spoke positively. "Storm will be fine. He'll get to play in the fields and go out on the trails. It's not a bad life."

"But it's not Storm, is it?" Daniel pointed out.

Amy didn't say anything.

"Hey," Daniel said, "just see how it goes. Things might be different next year, you might change your mind."

"Perhaps," Amy said, but she knew she wouldn't. If the choice was between shows and Heartland, then … well, there wasn't a choice.

Amy tried not to think about her decision. She found that if she concentrated on working then she could almost forget that she wasn't going in shows again. She could almost believe that next week, or the week after, she and Storm would be setting off in the trailer once again and that Storm would once again fly round a course of jumps. No one mentioned her decision to her, although on Tuesday night Lou did ask in an almost too-casual way if she had spoken to Tim since the weekend. Amy hadn't. She was dreading it. She knew how disappointed her dad was going to be when he heard the news.

Amy threw herself into her work. It wasn't hard to keep herself busy. For a start, she was determined to help Willow overcome her fear of noises.

"She can't keep panicking every time she hears something flap or bang," she said to Ty as they groomed the little bay pony the next day. "She'll never be safe to be ridden."

"I know," Ty said. He looked thoughtful. "How about we set up an obstacle course for her?"

"An obstacle course?" Amy echoed, wondering what he meant.

"You know, a selection of things that she might be nervous of – flags on sticks, cones, bags, plastic sacks. We probably won't be able to get her close to them at first but as she starts to realize that they're not going to hurt her then hopefully she should get more confident and eventually she should get so used to them that they won't bother her any more."

"It's a great idea," Amy said enthusiastically. "Let's try it this afternoon."

Over lunchtime, they set out a course of obstacles in one of the smaller paddocks – they put down a grid of poles, stuck a flag in a cone, found a bucket that could be rattled, put a plastic bag on a stick and put a sheet of plastic on the floor, weighted down with stones

"Come on, Willow," Amy said, leading Willow into the paddock after it was all set up.

Willow walked a few paces into the field and then stopped and stared at the obstacles. Amy stood beside her, stroking her neck and letting her take her time. "Nothing's going to hurt you," she told the pony. "I promise."

As Willow started to relax, Amy walked to the end of the lead-rope. She didn't pull Willow or hassle her. She just waited. After five minutes, Willow stepped forward of her own accord. Amy started to walk around the outside of the paddock. She held the lead-rope at the end and Willow followed her. Every time they had completed a circuit of the paddock, Amy led Willow just slightly closer to the obstacles. Occasionally Willow would tense nervously, then Amy would listen to her fear and let her stop. Each time, she waited calmly for Willow to relax again and then led her on.

After half an hour the pony was walking about eight feet away from the obstacles.

"I won't take her any closer today," Amy said to Ty, who was watching by the gate. "I don't want to push it too quickly and frighten her."

Ty nodded in agreement. "You've had an audience," he said, pointing to the next field.

Solitaire was watching curiously over the fence. Amy had a sudden idea. "I know Solly's not going to be backed for several years yet," she said, "but couldn't we do the obstacle course with him too? It'll be good for him to get used to things like this now. And he's so confident that I can't imagine he'll be fazed."

She was right. The next day Ty led the foal into the paddock alongside Willow. The youngster hardly even looked twice at the poles or the flag or the flapping plastic bag, although he did stick his head into the bucket to see if there was any food inside.

His confidence seemed to have a good effect on Willow. Seeing Solitaire exploring things so readily, the bay pony cautiously edged closer.

"That's great!" Ty said, as Willow walked up to the bucket and began to nose at it.

Amy nodded, delighted at Willow's new confidence. "Working the two of them together really seems to be doing the trick."

They let the two ponies touch noses. "They seem to like each other," Amy said. "Why don't we put them out in the same field? Now that Willow's reliable to catch, she doesn't need to be on her own any more."

"Good idea," Ty agreed.

After they had finished with the obstacle course, they

turned Solitaire and Willow out together. The two youngsters trotted away and settled down to graze.

"They look happy," Amy said.

Ty smiled. "They do." He took Amy's hand and they started to walk down the yard. "So, how are you feeling?" he asked.

"What do you mean?" Amy asked knowing full well he was talking about her decision not to compete Storm any more, but stalling for time.

"About Storm," Ty persisted. "Have you changed your mind?"

"No," Amy said, not wanting to talk about it. "But I'm fine about it."

*And is Storm?* a little voice asked in her head. She ignored it. Storm would be fine — he'd have to be.

To her relief, Ty dropped the subject.

As they reached the front stable block, there was a whinny. Amy looked round expecting it to be Storm, but to her surprise it wasn't. It was Duke. He was looking at Ty.

"Wow!" Amy said, astounded.

"He's been coming on really well," Ty said, going over to the big bay and patting him. "You were so right. There's not a mean bone in his body." Amy watched as Ty stroked Duke's nose. "I'm pretty sure he must have been treated well by his previous owners," Ty went on, "and that his only bad treatment was at Green Briar."

"Have you picked up his feet yet?" Amy asked.

"Not yet, but he'll let me touch his legs now," Ty said.

Just then, Ben came out of the tack-room with Red's travelling wraps.

"Have you got a moment to give me a hand loading Red, Amy?" he asked, seeing her standing there.

"Sure," she replied.

Ben was going to a local show that afternoon. She unbolted the ramp. It felt kind of strange that she wasn't going too, but at the same time she realized that she felt relieved. There was so much she wanted to do that afternoon – ride Dylan, groom Willow, spend some time with Sundance. She couldn't have done any of it if she'd been at the show.

Ben led Red down to the trailer. The handsome chestnut walked in eagerly and Amy heaved the ramp into place.

"Good luck," she said as Ben let himself out of the jockey door.

"It's only a small show," he said. "We're just going to go and have fun." He looked up the yard. "Looks like someone wishes he was coming too."

Amy followed his gaze. Storm was looking over his door. Nodding his head impatiently, he kicked his door, as if he was expecting to be put in the trailer too.

"See you," Ben said to Amy and got into the pick-up and started the engine. As the trailer moved off, Storm whinnied frantically.

Amy's heart clenched. It was obvious he wanted to go. He couldn't understand why he was being left behind.

"Hush now, boy," she said, going to his door. She stroked his face but he pulled away from her, his eyes fixed on the trailer. As it disappeared from view he whinnied again and again, and nothing Amy could do could soothe him.

She felt bad. She hated seeing him so upset.

"Storm, you can't go," she said. "We're not going to shows any more."

Storm whinnied again and the sound seemed to go straight through her. She couldn't bear to see him like this.

She looked towards the house and then headed for the phone.

"You want me to ride Storm in the show for you on Sunday?" Daniel echoed.

"Yes," Amy replied, her fingers gripping the receiver. "If you're free that day."

"I can do it, no problem," Daniel told her. "But I thought you said it wouldn't work, getting someone else to take Storm in shows."

"It won't. It's just this once," Amy said. "I feel awful. Storm saw Red going off to a show just now and he keeps whinnying. He doesn't understand why he's been left behind. He's going to be just the same on Sunday when Ben goes to the show then."

Daniel spoke slowly. "But what about the weekend after, when Ben goes to another show, or the weekend after that?"

Amy didn't want to think about it. "I'll think of something," she said. "I just need more time."

"OK," Daniel said. "Well, I'm more than happy to ride Storm for you on Sunday. What's he entered in?"

"The High Juniors," Amy said. "I can ring the show and swap your name for mine as the rider. You are still eighteen, aren't you?"

"Yes," Daniel replied. "So do you want me to come and collect Storm in my trailer?"

"It's all right," Amy replied. "I'm sure Ben won't mind taking him with Red. He's planning to get there about nine."

"OK, tell him I'll meet him by the secretary's tent at nine fifteen," Daniel said. "If he's going to be late he can ring me on my mobile." He paused. "You are sure about this, aren't you, Amy?"

"Yes," Amy insisted. She suddenly pictured Storm walking into the trailer, ready for the show, leaving her behind, and a tight band seemed to pull around her heart. She swallowed and forced the image away. "Yes," she repeated resolutely. "I'm sure."

# Chapter Nine

On Sunday morning Amy got up early to groom and braid Storm. "You be good, you hear," she said as she led him out of his stall.

Storm watched Red load into the trailer. He pawed at the ground impatiently and pulled towards the ramp, his ears pricked. He looked so eager, so excited.

Amy swallowed. "I won't be there, Storm, but I'll be thinking about you," she told him. "Jump well for Daniel."

Storm snorted and pushed at her impatiently with his head.

"OK," Ben called.

Amy led Storm up the ramp and tied him up, then gave him a last pat and slipped out through the jockey door. As she shut it she saw Storm and Red touch noses as though pleased that they were back together.

"Say good luck to Daniel for me," she said to Ben.

"I will," he promised, getting into the pick-up.

Amy watched as he started the engine and drove away. With a sigh, she turned and trudged up the yard to get on with the mucking out.

She tried hard to keep herself busy she couldn't stop thinking about Storm. *He'll have arrived at the show now*, she thought, looking at her watch as she went into the straw barn and seeing it was just after nine o'clock. *Ben's probably just unloading him. He'll be looking round. The jumps will be out in the ring...*

"Earth to Amy!" Lou waved a hand in front of her nose.

Amy jumped.

"That bale of straw's not going to get to the barn by itself," Lou commented.

"Sorry," Amy said, realizing that Lou was trying to get past her to pick up some clean straw.

"Thinking about Storm?" Lou asked.

Amy nodded and turned to pick up the bale.

"It must be tough for you." Lou spoke quietly. "But I do understand."

Amy stared.

"I know you think I don't love the horses like you do," Lou said, "and I guess I don't. But that doesn't stop me from being able to see what a difficult decision it must have been for you to give up shows. I can guess how hard it must be for you to think of Storm competing with someone else."

Amy didn't know what to say. She hadn't admitted to anyone how much she hated the thought of Storm going to a show without her. She knew it made her sound selfish and she was sure other people wouldn't understand. But Storm was just so precious to her.

"Look," Lou said gently, "what do you say we finish up the stalls and then take a drive up to the show? It'll only take us twenty minutes by car. If we move it we should get there in time to see Storm go in his class. We can come back straight afterwards so we won't lose much time here."

A smile broke out on Amy's face. "I'd like that. Thanks, Lou."

Her sister smiled back. "No problem."

They arrived at the showground just after ten. The show was in full swing. Hurrying through the crowds of people, they headed for the jumper ring.

"And next in class 31, we have number 266, Jane Simmons riding Hollow Deep Whisperer," a voice over the loudspeaker announced.

"That's my class," Amy said quickly.

"Look, there's Daniel!" Lou said, pointing to the collecting ring.

As Amy's eyes fell on Storm, her heart seemed to miss a beat. Daniel was riding him round the collecting ring. Storm's ears were pricked. Amy stopped, feeling suddenly strange. It was really weird to see Storm there without her.

He looked just like he always did at shows – happy and excited. *Well, how did you expect him to look?* she thought. Deep in her mind, she knew the answer. She'd wanted him to look different, to be quieter – to be missing her...

"Shall we go and say hi?" Lou said eagerly.

But suddenly Amy didn't want to. She shook her head. Seeing Lou's surprised expression she said quickly, "It ... it might upset Storm, it might make him lose concentration."

Lou shrugged. "Well, you know Storm best. We can say hello afterwards. Let's find a seat."

They sat down in the busy stands.

Amy sat forward on her seat, her arms hugging her stomach. She didn't say anything. Her eyes stared at the ring but she hardly even saw the horse who was jumping the course. All she could think about was Storm.

"That was four faults there for number 266, Jane Simmons on Hollow Deep Whisperer," the voice announced over the loudspeaker as the horse cantered out of the ring. There was a pause while the clapping died down and then the loudspeaker crackled into life again. "Next in class 31 we have number 125, Daniel Lawson riding Summer Storm."

Amy barely registered the polite clapping around her. Her eyes were fixed on Storm. He came trotting into the ring, his hooves flicking lightly across the grass, his head and neck flexed, his ears pricked in anticipation.

She saw Daniel lean forward and murmur something. Storm's ears flickered and he moved smoothly into his long-striding canter. Amy felt every hoofbeat, every ripple of his powerful muscles as he cantered around the ring.

The starting bell rang. Daniel stroked Storm's neck and then turned him into the first fence. Storm's ears pricked, his stride lengthened and they met it perfectly, flowing over it, moving as one.

Amy was spellbound. Lightly balanced on Storm's back, Daniel guided the grey gelding over jump after jump. They cleared each fence with inches to spare and suddenly Amy could see what so many people had been telling her. Storm wasn't just good — she knew that from watching him jump at home with Daniel — he was breathtaking. Out of the show ring he might be gentle and affectionate but in the show ring he became a different horse. Courage and strength seemed to shine out of his eager, willing eyes. He made you want to watch him. He made you believe he could jump the moon. And, more than that, Amy suddenly saw what Ben and Daniel had been trying to tell her. Storm loved the ring. It was his home.

As Storm jumped the last fence of the jump-off course and galloped through the finish with the fastest clear round of the competition so far, the crowd erupted into loud applause. Grinning broadly, Daniel patted Storm's neck and slowed him down from a gallop into a canter and finally into a trot. Storm tossed his head delightedly. He knew he'd done well.

"Amy!"

Amy barely registered her sister's voice. She watched as Daniel rode out of the ring. She could see the exhilaration on his face, see the happiness in Storm's eyes.

"Amy!" Lou put a hand on her arm. "Come on! Let's go and find them. That was an amazing round!"

Amy stood up as if in a dream. Her thoughts were spinning in her head.

She followed Lou out of the stand towards the collecting ring. Suddenly her heart clenched. There was Storm with Daniel. They looked so happy, so excited.

Amy stopped.

Lou looked at her. "What?" She seemed to see the paleness of Amy's face. "What is it?" she demanded.

Amy shook her head. "I ... I can't," she said. "I can't see them."

"But why?" Lou said.

Amy couldn't find the words. Her eyes begged Lou to understand.

Lou frowned in concern. "What's the matter, Amy?" she said solicitously.

Amy stared at Storm. "I just can't," she whispered. Her heart felt like it was going to break. Deep down, in the part of her that went beyond words, she knew what she was going to have to do. And she couldn't bear it. She just couldn't bear it.

"Please, Lou," she said, her voice trembling on the brink of tears. "I just want to go home."

To her relief, Lou didn't argue. She looked confused but she shrugged. "OK."

"Amy! Lou!"

Amy's heart plummeted. It was too late. Ben had seen them.

"Over here!" he called.

Lou looked at Amy, seeming to wonder what to do. Amy swallowed. There was no way out now. Taking a deep breath, she forced her legs to move.

"Hi," she called. To her ears, her voice sounded forced and strange. But Ben and Daniel didn't seem to notice.

"Hey there!" Ben said as they walked over. Storm whickered and raised his head.

"I didn't know you were coming to watch," Daniel said.

"It was an impulse decision," Lou said. Amy felt her sister glance at her as if expecting her to say something, but Storm was nuzzling at her hands and suddenly she found that she couldn't speak.

"We saw your round," Lou said quickly as if to fill the silence. "It was amazing!"

Daniel grinned and patted Storm. "It wasn't anything to do with me. Storm was awesome!" He looked at Amy. "You can't be serious about not competing with him, Amy."

"I am," she said. Tears pricked her eyes but once again no one seemed to notice.

"But he loves the ring," Daniel protested. "You can feel him change the second you ride through the gate. It's like he comes alive. You can't take that away from him."

"I know," Amy whispered. She stared at Storm's face, a lump swelling in her throat. She pushed the words painfully past it. "That's why..." She looked at Lou and took a deep breath. "That's why I think we should sell him."

"Sell him?" Ben echoed.

Feeling numb, Amy nodded. "If you agree, Lou," she said, her eyes on her sister's.

Lou stared at her in astonishment.

"I don't understand," Daniel said quickly. "Why do you feel you should sell Storm?"

Amy turned to him. "You said it yourself, Daniel. You said that Storm belongs in the show ring. Well, I saw that just now when you were riding him." She touched Storm's warm neck. "When Storm first came to Heartland I promised that his happiness would always come first. If we keep him I'll be breaking that promise."

"So we sell him and you become unhappy?" Lou said softly to her.

"If that's the way it has to be," Amy whispered, blinking back the tears.

"But there are other options," Daniel said quickly. "Doing this – getting someone else to ride him in shows..."

Amy was already shaking her head. "He deserves more than that. He needs someone who can spend time with him – at home and at shows. I can't give him the time he needs. Not with all the other horses to look after." Swallowing hard, she stroked Storm's face. "I wish I could, but I can't."

For a moment, no one spoke.

At last Ben sighed. "It's a big decision," he said.

Lou put an arm around Amy's shoulders. "Ben's right," she said quietly. "It is a big decision but I'm sure it's for the best."

"What will you do, Amy?" Daniel said. "Advertise him?"

"I guess," Amy replied. She hadn't thought beyond the decision. She looked at Lou. "Though I'll have to talk to Dad first. He might want to take him back."

"I don't think he will," Lou said. "He made it clear that Storm was a gift to us. But he might help us find a good home for him."

"I could spread the word around the show circuit, if you want?" Daniel said. "There'll be quite a few people interested in him. Particularly those who've seen him jump here today."

Amy nodded wordlessly and, after giving Storm one last pat, she turned and walked slowly to the car.

The moment Ty saw her getting out of the car at Heartland he realized that there was something badly wrong.

He put down the water bucket he was carrying and hurried over.

"I'll be in the house," Lou said and left Amy and Ty together.

"Amy, what is it?" Ty said, his eyes searching her face in alarm. "Has something happened to Storm?"

Amy shook her head. At the sight of his familiar face, all

the tears that she had been holding back spilled from her eyes.

Ty's arms enfolded her. "Amy?" he said as she began to cry. "What's wrong?"

"I don't want to sell him," she sobbed. "I don't want to."

"Sell who?" Ty questioned.

"Storm," Amy replied. "You should have seen him at the show. He looked so happy. It's not fair to keep him. He needs a home where he can compete. He can't stay here." Her voice choked on her tears. "I love him so much, Ty."

Ty kissed her hair. "I know you do," he said sadly. "So maybe selling him is for the best."

They stood there for half an hour, until at last Amy felt calm enough to think about the other horses. She set to work with a vengeance. She wanted to be busy. She wanted to have things to do to stop her thinking about Storm. Focusing intently on each job as she did it, she managed to push Storm to the back of her mind. But then Ben's trailer came up the drive.

As Ben lowered the ramp, Storm whinnied. Seeing his dark eyes and pricked ears, Amy's heart wanted to stop.

Ben handed his lead-rope to Amy along with a blue ribbon. "He won," he said.

Amy looked at the rosette for a moment then handed it back to Ben. "Daniel should have it." She swallowed hard and clicked her tongue. "Come on, Storm."

She led Storm to his stall. Touching his smooth shoulder, she tried to picture what it would be like to see him walking into a trailer as he left Heartland for the last time. How would she feel? But her mind went blank. It was as if she couldn't let herself imagine that. *This isn't happening*, she thought numbly. *This isn't real*.

Her sense of unreality continued. That evening she took the phone up to her room to make the call she'd been dreading.

"Amy," her dad said when he answered. "What a nice surprise!"

"Hi, Dad," Amy said quietly.

"How are you? Been up to anything exciting? How're Lou and Storm?"

"We're all fine." Amy hesitated. It was now or never. "Dad, I've … I've got something to tell you."

Her dad seemed to hear the seriousness in her voice. "What?"

"It's…" Amy paused. "It's Storm. Lou and I don't think we should keep him any more." As the words came out she felt hollow inside.

Tim sounded shocked. "But why?"

Amy explained how she couldn't compete and run Heartland, about how she couldn't bear to see Storm unhappy and know it was her doing. "It's not fair," she finished. "He'll be happier with someone else. Lou agrees with me." Tears sprang to her eyes. She blinked them away.

"Would you like him back? We know how valuable he is. You could sell him."

"No. He's your horse — yours and Lou's," Tim said. "You've done all the work on him and if you sell him then you should keep the money. But are you sure that selling him is the right decision? There must be another way."

"There isn't," Amy told him. "This is the only way Storm'll be really happy. He needs an owner who's got time for him — who can take him in shows."

Her father tried to suggest solutions that didn't involve selling Storm but in the end he reluctantly had to agree that selling Storm did seem to be the only option. "Oh, Amy," he said and she could hear the sadness in his voice. "I'd so hoped…" He broke off. "What matters now is that you and Lou do what you think is best."

Amy was sure he'd been going to say he'd hoped to see her become a showjumper like he and her mom had been. "I'm sorry, Dad," she said, feeling as if she had somehow let him down.

"Amy, sweetheart," Tim said, "you've got nothing to be sorry about. I know this must be really hard for you. But I gave Storm to you and Lou, and together you must decide what's best." He sighed. "Do you want me to help you find him a home?"

"Well, Daniel — my friend — is going to spread the words round the show circuit here," Amy said. "But if you hear of someone, I want Storm to go to a good home."

"I'll let you know straight away," Tim promised.

"I'd better go now," Amy said quietly.

"OK," Tim replied. He paused. "Amy…"

"Yes?" she said.

"I love you very, very much," he said. "Whatever you do, whatever choices you make, that will never change."

"Thanks, Dad," Amy managed to say. "I love you too. I'll speak to you soon."

Sinking on to the bed, she threw the phone down and put her head in her hands.

# Chapter Ten

*It's just a bad dream*, Amy thought as she woke up the next morning. *Storm isn't really going.* But her relief was swiftly replaced by an icy coldness as she realized that it wasn't a dream. She really was going to sell Storm.

She lay in bed wishing that time would stand still. But outside the horses were already starting to kick at their stall doors. She had to get up. They needed their breakfasts.

Amy dressed slowly. As she went outside, Ty pulled up in front of the house in his pick-up.

"How are you this morning?" he asked, looking at her in concern.

Amy shrugged. "I've been better."

Ty nodded understandingly. "Do you want to talk about it?"

Amy shook her head. There was nothing to say. She

looked at the stable block and saw Storm looking at her, his ears pricked. She swallowed and looked away.

Ty put an arm round her shoulders. "Come on," he said quietly. "Let's feed the horses."

Amy was in the middle of mucking out Jake's stall when the phone rang. She went down to the house to answer it.

"Heartland – Amy Fleming speaking," she said, her mind still half on the yard, thinking about what there was to do.

"Hi," a man said curtly. "My name's Buchanon, Charles Buchanon. I believe you've got a horse for sale. A grey gelding? Jumps in Juniors?"

For a moment, Amy was almost too shocked to speak. "Er … yes," she said. She collected herself quickly. "We haven't advertised him yet."

"I was at Marriott Park yesterday. I heard the guy riding him talking to some people. He said he was for sale."

"Yes, well, yes he is," Amy said, feeling slightly unreal.

"Great," the man said. "I've seen him jump several times. He's a talented horse. I should think several of my clients would be interested in buying him."

"Clients?" Amy said.

"I'm a horse dealer," Mr Buchanon said. "So, how much are you asking for him?"

Amy didn't know what to say. She hadn't even thought of a price. All she'd thought about was getting Storm a good home. "You're a dealer?"

"Yes, that's right," Mr Buchanon said. "What price do you want?"

"I'm sorry," Amy felt awkward but it was Storm's happiness that was at stake. "But he's not for sale to a dealer. I want to know what sort of home he's going to."

"I'll pay you cash," Mr Buchanon said, as if that was bound to change her mind.

"It doesn't matter," Amy said firmly. "Finding him a good home is more important than any amount of money — cash or otherwise. I'm sorry."

She replaced the receiver. She couldn't believe they'd had a call about Storm already. She'd have to talk to Lou about what sort of price they were going to ask for him. She felt sick at the thought. All she wanted was for Storm to be happy.

By mid-morning, three further people had telephoned about Storm. All of them had been unsuitable as far as Amy was concerned. Two of them had been more dealers and one had been the father of a child rider who had a string of ten horses.

"I don't want you to just be one of a group of horses looked after by stable-hands," she told Storm. "You deserve a home where there'll be someone who'll spend time with you — who'll really love you."

He snorted and tilted his face so she could scratch his forehead.

"You big softy," Amy told him, rubbing his head.

She looked at Ty. He was working with Duke on the yard.

Duke's ears flickered but he stood still as Ty ran a hand down his legs.

"He's looking good," Amy commented.

Ty nodded. "I want to try picking up one of his feet. Would you hold him for me? I don't want to keep him tied in case he pulls back."

"Sure." Amy went over and untied Duke.

"There's a good boy," Ty said, patting him. "Now let's just have a look in this foot." Running his hand down Duke's left foreleg, he clicked his tongue and leaned his weight slightly against Duke's shoulder. Duke raised his head anxiously but then he lifted his hoof just as Ty wanted.

"Good boy!" Ty exclaimed, holding the toe of the hoof just an inch or so off the ground.

Amy patted the gelding in delight.

Ty put Duke's hoof down and fed him a chunk of carrot. "Well, that seemed to go OK," he said. "I'll try a hind leg now."

Slowly he worked his way round the horse's other three hooves.

With every minute that seemed to pass, Duke seemed to relax more and soon he was willingly lifting all his hooves for Ty.

After Ty had worked his way round Duke's hooves twice, he stopped and frowned. "Something's not right, Amy."

"What do you mean?" she asked curiously.

Ty looked at Duke, "I don't understand why he was so bad at Green Briar. I mean, look at him now. He's lifting all his feet just fine. If he had been playing up because he had been genuinely scared, then there's no way I'd have got as far with him this quickly. I'd have expected to have stopped at just lifting one hoof a tiny way off the ground. But he's quite happy for me to pick his feet up."

"That's true," Amy said, understanding what he was getting at. She looked at Duke's relaxed face. "He doesn't seem fazed at all."

"He started playing up when the farrier came, didn't he?" Ty said.

Amy nodded. "Are you thinking he might be scared of being shod?"

"Maybe," Ty said. He frowned. "But then that wouldn't explain why he kept playing up when the farrier wasn't there."

"And the farrier didn't actually shoe him," Amy said, remembering what Daniel had told her. "He only got as far as lifting his foot on to the stand when Duke freaked." An idea came to her. "Maybe he's scared of the stand."

Ty didn't look convinced. "But then why would he play up the next day?"

"Yeah," Amy said realizing he was right.

"Hang on," Ty said suddenly. "It could be something to do with having his foot lifted on to the stand, though. Let's just try something."

He ran his hand down one of Duke's forelegs. Duke obediently picked up his hoof.

Very slowly and watching Duke's face, Ty pulled Duke's leg out to the front just as a farrier would do and started to lift it as if to put his hoof on a stand.

Duke immediately flung his head up, his muscles tensing in pain.

Instantly Ty put his foot down. "It's OK, boy."

Amy looked at Ty. "It hurts him!"

"He doesn't seem to have any obvious painful spots," Ty said, his fingers gently examining Duke's forelegs, chest and shoulders. The gelding didn't flinch. "It seems to be just when his foot is lifted out at that angle."

Amy thought back. "Could it have anything to do with the way Val Grant rushed him back into work?" she suggested. "Maybe it made those muscles sore."

Ty nodded. "I think I'll give Scott a call and see what he thinks." He patted Duke. "We'll sort you out, Duke. Don't worry."

Amy put Duke away in his stall while Ty phoned the vet.

She was refilling Duke's water bucket when Ty came out of the house. "What did he say?" she asked

"He's going to call in tomorrow, but he suggested it might be a good idea to get a chiropractor to see him," Ty replied.

"Does he know of one?" Amy asked.

"Yes, he gave me the name of a friend of his – Dr Max Barker."

"Are you going to call him?" Amy asked.

"I already have," Ty nodded. "He's in the area this afternoon. He said he'd stop by after lunch."

Dr Barker arrived just after two o'clock. He was a tall, thin man in his forties with a wide smile and thinning hair. Dressed in jeans, a T-shirt and trainers, he didn't look much like a horse vet, but as soon as he started working on Duke it was clear he knew exactly what he was doing.

He asked them what they knew about Duke's history and then watched the bay gelding moving. "OK," he said, nodding. "Now I'll just check him over."

Ty stroked Duke's face while the chiropractor felt and pressed Duke's back, hindquarters, shoulders and neck, a quizzical look on his face.

Within five minutes he was starting to nod.

"OK," he said at last, finishing his examination and patting Duke. "He's sore in his shoulders, withers and through his neck. His hips are a little painful too. From what you've told me, I'd say that the sudden onset of exercise after a prolonged lay-off caused most of his problems." He shook his head. "You can't expect a horse to come back to full work in a matter of weeks."

"Can you do anything to help him?" Amy asked.

"Sure," Dr Barker said. "I'd say three or four sessions over the next few weeks should do it."

"It'll make him better?" Ty said.

Dr Barker nodded. "Should make him as good as new."

Amy and Ty exchanged delighted glances.

Dr Barker patted Duke. "Come on, boy, let's get started." He began to gently manipulate Duke's neck and withers with his hands.

"So all Duke's problems were caused by Val," Amy said in disgust. "That woman!"

"Duke must have found it painful when the farrier tried to lift up his leg," Ty said. "No wonder he freaked out."

"And no wonder he wasn't keen on anyone picking up his legs after that," Amy said.

"Poor boy," Ty said, stroking Duke's face. "The only option you had was to try and escape by pulling back away from them and they beat you up for that. It's no wonder you resorted to biting and kicking."

Dr Barker looked round. "It's amazing how many so-called stubborn or bad horses are really just horses in pain," he said.

Amy nodded. It was something they saw over and over again at Heartland. Horses being labelled as difficult, when really all they were trying to do was to tell the humans looking after them that they were frightened or hurting. "If only people listened more to what horses were trying to say," she said wistfully.

Dr Barker nodded in agreement. "But then I see places like yours," he said looking round at Heartland, "and that gives me hope. We'll make a difference – those of us who care. It might take time but we'll get there."

Amy smiled. She liked Dr Barker more with every minute.

"Right, all done," he said at last. "I'll call back in two days, about the same time."

"That's great," Amy said. "And thank you."

While Ty put Duke away in his stall, Amy walked down to the Dr Barker's car with him. "See you on Wednesday," she called as he got into his Jeep and drove away.

Amy was about to go back to Ty when she stopped her in her tracks. A silver car was driving up the drive – a very smart Mercedes. Amy frowned. She knew that car. It was... She stared. It was the Grants'!

Amy watched in astonishment as Val drove up to about three feet away from her and stopped the engine.

Ashley was sitting in the passenger seat. She didn't get out. She didn't even look at Amy.

Val Grant opened her door. "Hello, Amy." She smiled.

Amy's skin immediately prickled with distrust. Why was she acting like they were friends?

"What do you want, Mrs Grant?" she asked.

Val Grant got out of the car. "I was wondering if your sister or grandfather were about."

"No, they're not; they're both out," Amy said.

"Pity." Val Grant looked slightly taken aback. "Well," she said, "maybe you can help. I hear Storm's for sale."

Amy stared at her.

"I'd be interested in buying him," Val Grant continued briskly. "That's why I wanted to see your sister or grandfather. To discuss a price. You've done quite well with him, considering."

"Considering what?" Amy demanded, her hackles starting to rise.

"Well…" Val looked round meaningfully at Heartland's barns and fields. "This isn't exactly the place for a horse of Storm's abilities, is it, Amy? Even you can see that. He's got real talent."

A wave of anger rose up inside Amy. "So you think he'd be better off with you, do you?" she said.

Val Grant looked at her as if she was crazy. "Well, obviously. You only have to look at the facilities we have at Green Briar – and, of course, he'd get a rider whose abilities matched his own."

Struggling to control herself, Amy said coldly, "I think you should leave now, Mrs Grant. We're not going to sell Storm to you."

"I see." Val Grant smiled at her as if she were a child. "Look, maybe I should be discussing this with your grandfather."

"The answer will still be no," Amy said. "I have the final say on where Storm goes."

"I'm willing to pay a very good price," Val said.

Amy couldn't believe that Val didn't get it. "It doesn't matter how much you'll pay," she said. "There's no way I'm selling him to you."

At that moment, Duke put his head over his stall door.

Val stared as if she couldn't believe her eyes. "That horse!" she exclaimed, momentarily forgetting about Storm. "What's he doing here? I sold him to Daniel Lawson!"

"Yes. Daniel bought him for us," Amy said. "We're helping him."

Val Grant snorted in disbelief. "Then you're even more dumb than I thought. *Helping* him? There's only one place for a horse like that! He's crazy. Take my advice – what he needs is a bullet through the head."

Amy finally snapped. "Or someone who can help him with the pain he's in!" she said furiously. "The only reason Duke acts crazy is because his muscles are sore and it hurts him when he has his feet picked up. And that's because of how you worked him at Green Briar. You brought him back to full work in two weeks – didn't you think he might feel sore? When he started playing up didn't you think to check?"

She saw the initial surprise turn to anger. "What do you know?" Val demanded. "You know nothing about what I did with that horse. About how I tried to cure him."

"By shooting him with a pellet gun?" Amy said.

Val Grant's face stiffened. She stared at Amy for a moment and then swung round and walked back to her car.

"And you want me to sell you Storm?" Amy said. "He'll never go to a barn like yours. I should report you to the ASPCA."

Val Grant stopped in the middle of shutting her car door. "You can be as high and mighty as you like, Amy Fleming, but when that horse leaves here you've got no say over his future. No say at all."

She slammed the car door shut and drove away. Ashley hadn't looked at Amy once.

Amy stared after them, acknowledging the truth in Val's last words. Once Storm left Heartland, she would have no say in his life. Show horses were bought and sold all the time. What if he ended up in a bad home?

She walked up to Storm's stall and looked over his door. He was lying down. He nickered softly when he saw her.

Amy went into the stall and knelt down beside him. He nuzzled her knees and she felt a wave of despair sweep over her. "I don't know what to do," she whispered, feeling suddenly panicky. "I just don't know what to do."

The phone started to ring. Knowing that Ty and Ben were up in the top paddocks, Amy kissed Storm and reluctantly got up. She didn't feel like answering the phone. It would probably just be another call about Storm, but it might be an emergency — a phonecall about a horse who needed their help. She couldn't ignore it.

She ran to the house and picked up the phone.

"Hi, Amy." It was Nick Halliwell.

"Nick, hi!" Amy spoke with a rush of relief as she realized that it wasn't a phonecall about Storm.

"You sound very pleased to hear from me," Nick said, sounding surprised.

"No, it's just I thought you were going to be another person calling about Storm," Amy explained.

"Well," Nick said. "Actually, that's why I am calling. Have you sold him yet?"

Amy frowned in confusion. "No. Why?"

"Because I'd like to buy him."

Amy was too shocked to speak.

"Amy?" Nick said when she didn't say anything.

"You want to buy Storm!" Amy stammered.

"Definitely," Nick replied. "I think he's got tremendous talent and ability."

"You'd showjump him?" Amy said.

"No," Nick's voice had a smile in it. "I'd take him in barrel-racing competitions. What do you think, Amy? Of course I'd jump him."

"But… Well, I just never expected it," she stammered.

"I mean, I wouldn't jump him that much to start with," Nick said. "I'm often away at shows, which means my young horses are generally ridden by my working pupils – each of them is designated two or three horses to work with."

"Yes, I know," Amy said remembering her conversation with Daniel about it.

"I heard how well he jumped for Daniel yesterday," Nick

went on, "and what I'd like to do, if I do buy him, is to make Daniel his designated rider. That would mean Daniel would be in charge of overseeing his progress, looking after him, schooling him and riding him in shows while he progresses up through the grades."

Amy could hardly contain her delight. "That would be perfect!"

"So, how much are you asking for him?" Nick asked.

Amy told him the figure she and Lou had agreed.

"That sounds reasonable," Nick said. "So you'll consider selling him to me?"

"Yes," Amy said. A thought struck her. "You won't sell him on, though, will you, Nick?"

Nick paused. "I can't guarantee that I'll keep him for ever," he said honestly. "I haven't got space to keep horses who don't perform or reach their potential."

"Oh," Amy said, feeling her excitement deflate slightly. It had all seemed so perfect.

"But," Nick went on. "I'm sure we could come to some arrangement whereby I offer you first option on buying him back if I ever do decide to sell him on."

Amy felt a wave of relief. "I'll have to discuss it with Lou and Grandpa," she said, "but I think that sounds great."

As if on cue, she heard Grandpa and Lou arrive home with the groceries. "Can I call you back in ten minutes or so?" she said to Nick.

"Sure," he said.

* * *

"So what do you think?" she asked Grandpa and Lou after she'd told them about Nick's offer.

Grandpa sat down at the table. "It sounds very fair," he said.

"And Nick's so nice," Lou said. "It would be lovely for Storm to go to a showjumping home like that — and to be looked after by Daniel."

Amy nodded. She knew Daniel would take care of Storm as well as if he were his own horse.

"I think it's a great idea," Lou said. "And he wouldn't be too far away."

"I'll go and ring Nick back," Amy said. She went into the office and punched in Nick's number.

He answered the phone almost immediately. He was delighted when he heard the news. "That's great," he said. "In that case I'll send Daniel over for him as soon as possible."

Amy felt a shock run through her. This was real. Storm was actually going to leave Heartland. Daniel was going to come and collect him and take him away.

"Would tomorrow morning be any good?" Nick continued. "I'm leaving for a show in Germany on Wednesday and I'd really like to be here when he arrives."

Amy felt sick. "Yes," she heard herself saying. "Yes, tomorrow morning would be fine."

"Great," Nick said. "Daniel will be with you about ten."

Amy slowly put the phone down. She went into the kitchen and looked at Grandpa and Lou in a daze.

"Are you OK?" Lou asked.

"Daniel's coming for Storm tomorrow morning," Amy said. Her words sounded strange and distant, almost as if someone else was speaking them.

"That soon?" Grandpa said in surprise.

Lou came over to her. "I'm sure Nick will understand if you want to keep Storm a couple of weeks longer," she said, looking at her sympathetically.

"It's OK," Amy said. "I've … I've said it's fine."

She left the kitchen and walked up the yard. Hearing her footsteps, Storm came to his door and whinnied.

"Hey, boy," she whispered. She walked over to him, her eyes scanning every inch of his handsome face. She loved him so much and tomorrow he was going away. Feeling like her heart was being squeezed in a vice, she rested her forehead against his nose. He snorted softly. She stood there for a moment and then taking a deep breath, she forced herself to carry on up the yard to tell Ty and Ben the news.

They were in the feed-room measuring out the evening feeds.

"It'll be good for Daniel," Ben said, when she told them about Nick's phonecall.

Amy nodded wordlessly.

"And you'll be able to visit Storm loads," Ben went on.

Amy inwardly flinched. *Visit Storm*… But he was hers.

"How are you feeling about it?" Ty asked.

Amy nodded. "OK," she said, her voice high and tight.

"I ... I'm OK." She hesitated. "I think I'll go and start sweeping the yard," she said.

She walked off. The world seemed slightly blurred, as if she was somehow out of speed with it. She picked up a yard brush and began to sweep.

After everyone had gone that night, Amy fetched Storm's tack from the tack-room. She brushed him over and saddled him without a word. Seeming to sense something was wrong, Storm nuzzled her arm as she put the reins over his head.

She couldn't speak. She stroked his face.

*Tomorrow...* she thought, but once again her mind seemed to hit a blank wall.

Feeling empty inside, she led him out of the stall and mounted. The evening sunlight was soft, birds sang in the branches of the nearby trees. Not to ride Storm again, not to see him in his stall, not to hear his whinny. How could she bear it?

*I can't*, she thought simply.

Shortening her reins, she rode him out on to the trail that led up the hillside behind Heartland. He walked out, his stride swinging, his ears pricked.

As the trail entered the trees, Amy let him move into a trot and then a canter. She leant forward, feeling his powerful muscles move beneath her, feeling the wind in her face, and suddenly she was filled with the desire to ride him on and on, far away from Heartland and the coming morning. It could be just the two of them together.

*On and on*, she thought as his hooves thudded rhythmically into the grass. Her mind cleared as, for one blissful moment in time, she let herself believe it. *On and on. For ever.*

As the trail started twisting and turning, Storm slowed down, and, as he did so, reality flooded back. Amy drew him back to a walk and sadly patted his neck, acknowledging what she knew. There was going to be no for ever for her and Storm.

Amy slept badly that night. She got up early and was already feeding the horses when Ty arrived.

"Look, why don't you spend time with Storm this morning?" Ty said to her. "Ben and I can do the stalls."

"I can help too."

Amy turned. Lou was coming out of the house, her short blonde hair still ruffled from sleep. "Ty's right," Lou said. "You need to be with Storm."

"Thanks," Amy said quietly.

She fetched Storm's grooming kit and halter and set to work grooming him. She felt as if all her actions were slower than usual. *This is the last time*, she thought with every brush stroke. *The last time I'll be grooming him.*

But there was a bit of her that didn't quite believe it. And it wasn't until Nick's trailer came rattling up the drive that finally Amy knew it was true.

"Amy," Daniel said, getting out of the pick-up and coming to meet her.

"Hi," she said in a small voice.

Daniel's eyes searched her face. "I don't know what to say. I'm really pleased that Nick's buying Storm but I know how bad this must be for you."

"I'd rather you and Nick had him than anyone else," Amy said.

Their eyes met.

"I'll ... I'll go get him ready," Amy said.

"Amy, wait," Daniel said as she set off to the tack-room. "Nick sent some travel wraps. He thought it would save bringing yours back."

"Oh, right," Amy said, stopping.

Daniel fetched the wraps. "Do you want a hand?"

Amy shook her head.

"I'll just go and say hi to the others," Daniel said understandingly. "Just give me a shout when you're ready."

Amy walked slowly up to Storm's stall. Seeing the wraps in her arms, he nickered excitedly. Amy felt her heart twist. "You're not going to a show, boy," she said.

But Storm didn't understand. He pawed the ground eagerly.

Taking a deep breath, Amy crouched down and began to fasten Nick's wraps.

All too soon, Storm was ready.

"All done," Amy said, as she straightened up after fastening the last Velcro strap. Her throat felt tight. She walked over to Storm's head and kissed his face. For a moment she closed her eyes. "I'm doing this for you," she whispered. "For you, Storm."

Taking a deep breath she opened her eyes and went to the door. "Daniel!" she called, trying to keep her voice steady. "Storm's ready to go."

She went back to Storm and untied him. "I love you," she told him desperately. "Just remember that. No one could ever love you more." Hot tears filled her eyes.

Hearing footsteps on the yard she quickly brushed her tears away and, swallowing hard, led Storm out on to the yard.

"Hi, Storm," Daniel said patting him.

Ben, Ty and Lou came over.

"You be good for Daniel, Storm," Lou said to the grey gelding.

"Just don't go beating me and Red in any shows," Ben said, rubbing the gelding's face.

"Bye, Storm," Ty said softly.

Daniel glanced at Amy. "Do you want to lead him into the trailer? Or shall I?"

Amy hesitated. "You do it," she said, passing over the lead-rope.

Daniel took it and Storm walked forward eagerly. Amy watched. This couldn't be happening. Storm couldn't really be about to leave.

Storm reached the trailer. Suddenly Amy couldn't bear it any longer. She ran forward, putting her hand on his neck.

"Amy?" Daniel said.

Amy's chest rose and fell. How could she do this?

*I can't,* she thought desperately to herself. *I can't.* Just then, Storm pulled eagerly towards the trailer.

Looking at his pricked ears, Amy drew in a trembling breath and, using every ounce of willpower she possessed, she slowly took her hand from his neck.

"Love him for me, Daniel," she pleaded, her voice barely a whisper.

"Always," Daniel said, holding her gaze.

Amy stepped back, her jaw shaking with the effort of holding back the sobs that were threatening to overwhelm her.

"I'll ring you when we get to Nick's," Daniel said quietly as he put the ramp up.

Amy nodded, unable to speak.

As the trailer drove slowly away, a tear trickled down her cheek and then another. She heard footsteps behind her and then she felt Ty take her hand.

"You've done the right thing," he told her, his fingers gripping hers.

Amy shook her head wordlessly, her face now streaming with tears.

"Look around you, Amy," Ty said.

Amy glanced round at the yard, wondering what she was

supposed to be looking at. Lou and Ben were standing by Willow, who was tied up. In the distance the other horses and ponies were grazing in the fields.

"You couldn't have given this up," Ty said intensely. "I know losing Storm was hard, Amy, but you'll still be able to see him. Giving up Heartland would have meant giving up your heart."

A sob burst from Amy and she buried her head against his chest. Ty was right but, just at that moment, she couldn't think of anything but Storm.

Wrapping his arms around her, Ty let her cry for all she had lost.

As her sobs gradually quietened down, Amy lifted her head. As she looked again at the sunny yard and the peaceful horses, Ty kissed her forehead. In that instant she knew that she had made the right choice – for Storm, for the horses who needed her at Heartland, and for herself.

Looking into Ty's eyes, she saw her future.

"Everything will be OK," he whispered, pulling her close.

Amy smiled through her tears. "I know," she said, and, warm in his embrace, she meant it.